UNSILENCED

A JOURNEY OF SELF-DISCOVERY

JANET GARCIA

For permissions requests, speaking inquiries, and bulk order purchase options, email: publishing@uconcept.com.

ISBN: 978-1-960188-38-0 | E-book

ISBN: 978-1-960188-39-7 | Paperback

Published by Unlimited Concepts, Coconut Creek, Florida.

www.publishing.uconcept.com

Book, Editing, and Cover Design by Janet M Garcia | UConceptDesigns.com

Published in the United States of America.

To every teenager who has ever felt silenced, unseen, or unworthy—this book is for you.

To those who have faced the cruelty of bullying, whether from family members or peers, and have struggled to find their voice—I see you. You are stronger than you know, and your voice matters more than you can imagine.

This journey of self-discovery is yours to take, and along the way, may you find the courage to speak your truth, the strength to stand tall, and the love of true friends who uplift and support you.

You are not alone. You are worthy. You are unsilenced!

CONTENTS

1. Bullied and Broken   9

2. A New Classmate   19

3. Stepping Out of the Shadows   31

4. A Chance Encounter   43

5. A Supportive Friendship   57

6. Stepping Into the Spotlight   75

7. Confronting the PastIn the face of her brothers' cruelty, Janet's theater friends had chosen to offer her the very thing she had craved for so long - a sense of belonging, to be accepted, and their support.   89

8. Finding Forgiveness   103

9. Embracing the Spotlight   119

10. Reclaiming Her Voice   135

11. A Transformative Journey   149

12. Inspiring Others   165

13. Embracing the Future   181

14. Epilogue - A Lasting Impact   195

About the Author   217

BULLIED AND BROKEN

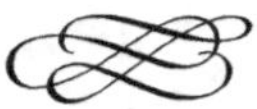

anet's eyes fluttered open, and a familiar sense of dread settled in the pit of her stomach. Another day of school, another day of facing the cruel taunts and judgmental stares that had become a constant in her life.

With a heavy sigh, she pushed herself up from the bed, her gaze immediately drawn to the mirror on the opposite wall. Janet's eyes scanned her reflection, scrutinizing every curve and imperfection. She was slightly overweight, a fact that her brothers never failed to remind her of with their merciless jabs and snide comments.

Memories of their cruel laughter echoed in her mind, like a relentless soundtrack that had become the backdrop to her daily existence. Janet winced, her fingers trailing over the soft flesh of her arms as she tried to find an outfit that wouldn't accentuate her insecurities.

The familiar ache of self-consciousness weighed heavily on her, a burden she had carried for as long as she could remember. No matter how hard she tried to blend in, to make herself smaller and less noticeable, the taunts and the laughter always found a way to cut her deep, chipping away at the fragile remnants of her self-esteem.

With trembling hands, she selected a loose-fitting sweater and a pair of dark jeans, hoping they would provide a measure of protection against the scrutinizing eyes of her peers. As she dressed, she couldn't help but steal one last glance at the mirror, wishing she could see the confidence and strength that others seemed to possess so effortlessly.

But all she saw was a girl trapped in a body she didn't recognize, a girl whose voice had been silenced by the relentless barrage of cruelty and judgment. Janet swallowed hard, steeling herself for the challenges that lay ahead, and made her way downstairs, bracing for another day of trying to survive the unforgiving social environment of high school.

The familiar scent of bacon and eggs wafted through the kitchen, but Janet's stomach churned with a mixture of anxiety and dread as she made her way to the breakfast table. Settling into her usual seat, she kept her gaze fixed on the plate in front of her, hoping to avoid the scrutinizing eyes of her brothers.

"Well, well, if it isn't our little piglet," her older brother, Michael, sneered, his lips curling into a cruel smile. "Did you have trouble fitting into your clothes this morning, sis?"

She felt her cheeks flush with embarrassment as the other brother erupted into laughter, their taunts echoing through the room. She shrunk down in her chair, wishing she could disappear into the floor and escape the relentless barrage of insults.

Her parents, engrossed in their own conversations and concerns, seemed oblivious to the tension that hung thick in the air. Janet's father sipped his coffee, while her mother busied herself with preparing the morning meal, their attention focused elsewhere.

Swallowing hard, Janet pushed the food around on her plate, her appetite vanishing in the face of her brothers' cruel words. She longed for the comfort and support that should have come from her family, but instead, she retreated further into the safety of her own thoughts, erecting invisible walls to shield herself from the pain.

In the silence that followed, Janet could hear the muffled laughter of her siblings, a constant reminder of her own perceived flaws and shortcomings. She blinked back the tears that threatened to spill, determined not to give them the satisfaction of seeing her break down.

As the breakfast table erupted in chatter once more, Janet's mind drifted to a world where she felt accepted and valued, a world where she didn't have to fear the judgment of those closest to her. But for now, she was trapped in a reality where her own family seemed intent on chipping away at her self-worth, leaving her to navigate the challenges of the day alone. Clutching the worn strap of her backpack, she made her way to the bus stop, her steps heavy with the weight of dread. As she boarded the crowded vehicle, she scanned the rows of seats, searching for an empty spot where she could tuck herself away, unnoticed.

Spotting an isolated seat near the back, Janet hurried towards it, her shoulders hunched in a futile attempt to make herself smaller. She sank down, pressing her back against the window, and fixed her gaze on the passing scenery, desperate to avoid the curious stares of her fellow passengers.

All around her, the bus erupted with the laughter and chatter of her classmates, their voices blending into a cacophony that only served to heighten Janet's sense of isolation. She listened as they swapped stories and made plans, their carefree interactions, a stark contrast to the turmoil churning within her.

Feeling like an outsider looking in, Janet's heart raced with a familiar anxiety. She knew that once they reached the school, the scrutiny and the judgment would only intensify, and the thought of facing another day of trying to blend into the background filled her with a sense of overwhelming despair.

Janet's fingers fidgeted with the hem of her sweater, a nervous habit she had developed over the years as a means of self-soothing. She took a deep, steadying breath, willing her body to calm, even as her mind raced with a thousand worries about the challenges that lay ahead.

The bus lurched forward, and Janet watched the familiar scenery blur past her window, her gaze unfocused as she lost herself in a sea of introspection. In these quiet moments, she allowed herself to dream of a world where she could walk with her head held high, free from the burden of self-consciousness and the fear of ridicule.

But as the bus neared the school, that fragile sense of hope began to crumble, and she steeled herself for another day of navigating the unforgiving social environment that had become her daily reality. The familiar sound of the school bell echoed through the halls, and Janet reluctantly made her way to her first-period class, her mind already consumed by a swirling mix of anxiety and dread.

As she slipped into her seat, she could feel the weight of her classmates' gazes upon her, and she fought the urge to shrink down, desperate to avoid drawing any unwanted attention. Janet's fingers gripped the edge of her desk, her knuckles turning white as she struggled to focus on the lesson unfolding before her.

The teacher's voice droned on, and Janet found herself drifting in and out of the discussion, her mind preoccupied with the overwhelming need to remain invisible. When the teacher suddenly called on her, she felt her heart leap into her throat, her mouth going dry as all eyes turned in her direction.

"Janet, can you tell us the answer to the question?"

Janet's mind raced, and she knew the answer, but the words caught in her throat, her lips trembling with the weight of her insecurities. She could feel the curious stares of her classmates burning into her, and the familiar sensation of panic began to rise within her.

"I-I'm sorry, I don't know," she stammered, her gaze fixed firmly on the surface of her desk.

The teacher nodded, seemingly unsurprised by Janet's response, and moved on to call on a more confident student, whose hand had shot up eagerly. Janet watched as the other student answered the question with ease, a mix of envy and relief washing over her.

While her classmates engaged in the discussion, Janet retreated further into herself, her mind a whirlwind of self-doubt and the persistent fear of being singled out. She knew the answers, but the thought of drawing attention to herself was simply too over-whelming to bear.

As the class wore on, Janet was lost in a sea of her own thoughts, her focus drifting away from the lesson and towards the ever-present desire to disappear, to become a silent observer in the world around her. It was a familiar coping mechanism, one that had become a well-worn path in the face of the constant judgment and ridicule she faced. The cafeteria bustled with activity as Janet made her way through the crowded room, her eyes scanning the sea of faces for a quiet corner where she could retreat. Spotting an unoccupied table in the far back, she quickly claimed the solitary seat, her movements almost mechanical as she set down her tray and settled in.

Around her, the lunchroom erupted with the laughter and chatter of her peers, their carefree interactions a stark contrast to the turmoil that churned within Janet. She watched as they clustered into tight-knit groups, sharing stories and inside jokes, and she couldn't help but feel a pang of longing, a deep desire to be a part of something, to belong.

But the fear of rejection, the persistent dread of being the target of ridicule, kept Janet firmly rooted in her isolated corner, her gaze downcast as she picked at the food on her tray. The aroma of freshly baked pizza and the sound of clattering trays only served to heighten her sense of isolation, a constant reminder of the gulf that separated her from her classmates.

Just as Janet was about to take a bite, a movement in her peripheral vision caught her attention. A girl from her English class, whose name Janet couldn't quite recall, offered her a tentative smile and a friendly wave. Janet felt a spark of hope flicker to life within her, and she mustered a small, hesitant smile in return, her heart swelling with the unexpected gesture of kindness.

But the moment of connection was shattered in an instant as a familiar voice rang out across the cafeteria.

"Well, well, isn't it our little piggy, enjoying her lunch all by herself?," Janet's brother, Michael, sneered, his words dripping with malice.

The laughter that erupted from his table cut through Janet like a knife, and she felt the color drain from her face as all eyes turned in her direction. The brief moment of hope that had blossomed within her now crumbled to dust, leaving her once again adrift in a sea of self-consciousness and shame.

Blinking back tears, Janet kept her gaze fixed on her tray, her appetite vanishing as the cruel laughter echoed through the cavernous room. In that moment, she wished she could simply disappear, to melt into the shadows and escape the relentless torment that had become the soundtrack to her life. As the final bell of the day rang, signaling the start of gym class, Janet felt a familiar sense of dread wash over her. She had always dreaded this particular period, a time when her physical insecurities were laid bare for all to see and judge.

Reluctantly, Janet changed into her gym clothes, her fingers trembling as she tied the laces of her worn sneakers. She knew what was coming – the dreaded team selection, where she would inevitably be the last one chosen, a constant reminder of her perceived shortcomings.

When the coach blew the whistle, signaling the start of the activity, Janet's heart raced as the students divided into two teams. She watched, her stomach in knots, as her classmates eagerly vied for the attention of the team captains, each one desperate to be selected first.

And then, it was Janet's turn. As her name was called, she felt the weight of her peers' scrutinizing gazes upon her, the snickers and whispers cutting deep. She shuffled forward, her head bowed, and took her place on the team that had been left with no other choice.

As the game commenced, Janet found herself on the sidelines, her attempts to participate met with eye rolls and sighs from her more athletic teammates. She tried to muster the courage to join the fray, to prove her worth, but the fear of failure and the sting of rejection held her back, cementing her position as the outsider, the one who didn't quite fit in.

With each passing minute, Janet's feelings of inadequacy grew, a heavy burden that threatened to crush her spirit. She watched as the others moved with a grace and confidence that she could only dream of, their laughter and camaraderie a stark contrast to the isolation that enveloped her.

In that moment, Janet felt like a ghost, a mere spectator in a world that seemed to have no place for her. The sting of her classmates' dismissive reactions echoed in her mind, a constant reminder of the barriers she had yet to overcome.

As the game drew to a close, Janet trudged off the court, her head bowed, the weight of her failure heavy on her shoulders. She knew that this was just the latest in a long line of humiliations, a cycle that seemed destined to repeat itself until she could find the strength to break free. The bell rang, signaling the end of the school day, Janet hurried out of the gymnasium, desperate to escape the lingering stares and whispers of her classmates. She knew that if she took the direct route home, she would inevitably cross paths with her brothers, and the thought of enduring another round of their cruel taunts was more than she could bear.

Quickening her pace, Janet veered off the main path, opting for a longer, more circuitous route that would allow her to avoid her siblings and the torment they inflicted. The familiar streets were quieter, the sounds of the school's bustling activity fading into the distance, and Janet felt a sense of relief wash over her.

In the solitude of her solitary walk, she allowed her mind to drift, indulging in a rare moment of daydreaming. Janet imagined a life where she felt confident and accepted, where her insecurities and the constant fear of ridicule no longer weighed her down. She pictured herself moving through the world with a sense of purpose and self-assurance, her voice heard and her unique qualities celebrated.

The wistful fantasy provided a temporary respite from the harsh realities of her daily existence, and Janet found herself walking with a slight spring in her step, her shoulders a little less hunched. For a fleeting moment, she felt a glimmer of hope, a tantalizing glimpse of the person she longed to become.

But as the familiar sight of her house came into view, Janet's fragile sense of peace shattered, and the weight of her burdens came crashing back down upon her. She steeled herself, bracing for the inevitable confrontation with her brothers, her heart racing with a familiar anxiety.

The closer she drew to the front door, the more Janet's steps slowed, her mind racing with a thousand scenarios of how the evening might unfold. Would her brothers be waiting, ready to pounce on her vulnerability? Would her parents even notice the tension, or would they remain oblivious to the turmoil that consumed their daughter?

With a deep, steadying breath, Janet reached for the doorknob, her fingers trembling as she prepared to face the next round of torment that awaited her within the walls of her own home. The moment Janet stepped through the front door, the familiar sounds of her brothers' laughter and taunts assaulted her senses, sending a wave of dread coursing through her. Without a word, she hurried up the stairs, her feet carrying her swiftly to the sanctuary of her bedroom, where she could finally escape the relentless torment.

Closing the door behind her, Janet leaned back against the solid wood, her chest heaving with the effort of holding back the tears that threatened to spill. She surveyed the familiar surroundings – the bookshelves overflowing with her favorite novels, the soft glow of the string lights that hung across the ceiling, the well-worn playlists on her phone – and was relieved.

This was her haven, a place where she could find solace and respite from the cruel realities of the outside world. Sinking down onto the edge of her bed, Janet reached for the worn copy of her favorite book, its pages witnessing the countless times she had sought refuge within its pages.

As she lost herself in the story, Janet allowed her mind to drift, imagining herself as the brave, confident heroine who faced her challenges with courage. She longed to embody that same sense of strength and self-assurance, to shed the heavy mantle of insecurity that had weighed her down for so long.

But just as she was beginning to feel a glimmer of hope, a tentative knock at her door shattered the illusion, pulling her back to the harsh realities of her life.

"Janet?" her mother's voice called out, laced with a hint of concern. "Can I come in for a moment?"

Reluctantly, Janet set the book aside, her fingers trembling as she reached for the doorknob. She knew her mother meant well, but the thought of opening up and revealing the depths of her struggles was a daunting prospect, one that she had long since learned to avoid.

As the door swung open, Janet's mother stepped inside, her expression a mix of empathy and worry. For a moment, they stood in silence, the air thick with unspoken emotions, and Janet felt the walls she had so carefully constructed begin to tremble, the weight of her burdens threatening to overwhelm her.

But before she could find the words to express the turmoil that consumed her, Janet retreated once more, retreating behind the safety of her carefully crafted defenses, unwilling to risk the vulnerability that true connection would require.

A NEW CLASSMATE

Janet's fingers gripped the worn strap of her backpack as she stepped into the familiar classroom, her gaze instinctively scanning the sea of faces. The familiar hum of chatter and laughter filled the air, a stark contrast to the turmoil churning within her.

Her eyes landed on a new figure standing beside the teacher's desk, and Janet felt her heart skip a beat. The boy, with his kind eyes and easy smile, was a stark contrast to the sea of familiar, judgmental faces that surrounded her. As the teacher introduced him as Liam, a transfer student, Janet felt a surge of anxiety wash over her.

Sinking into her usual seat, Janet's mind raced with a thousand worries. She couldn't help but notice that Liam was the only other student without a partner for the upcoming project, and a sense of dread settled in the pit of her stomach. The mere thought of being paired with him, of having to interact and potentially face rejection, was enough to make her palms grow clammy.

Janet silently prayed that the teacher wouldn't call on them, that somehow, miraculously, Liam would find a partner and she could retreat back into the safety of her own solitary existence. But as the teacher's voice rang out, shattering the relative calm, Janet felt her heart leap into her throat.

"Alright, class, for this next project, I'll be pairing you up. Let's see, Liam, why don't you work with Janet?"

The words hung in the air, and Janet could feel the weight of her classmates' curious gazes upon her. She risked a glance in Liam's direction, bracing herself for the familiar look of disappointment or disgust that so often graced the faces of her peers.

But to her surprise, Liam's expression remained warm and welcoming, his lips curving into a gentle smile as he made his way towards her desk. Janet felt her shoulders instinctively hunch, a futile attempt to make herself smaller, as Liam approached.

"Hi, Janet," he said, his voice soft and reassuring. "I'm looking forward to working with you on this project."

Janet's mouth felt dry, and she struggled to find the words to respond. The familiar sensation of panic began to rise within her, and she could feel the familiar sting of self-consciousness creeping up her neck.

"I-I, um, yeah, okay," she managed to stammer, her gaze fixed firmly on the surface of her desk.

As Liam settled into the seat beside her, Janet couldn't help but steal a quick glance in his direction, her heart racing with a mixture of trepidation and a tiny spark of curiosity. There was something about his demeanor, his genuine warmth, that caught her off guard, shattering the preconceptions she had so carefully constructed over the years.

But even as that glimmer of hope flickered to life, the familiar voice of self-doubt whispered in the back of her mind, reminding her that it was only a matter of time before Liam, like so many others, realized the truth – that she was simply not worth the effort.

As the teacher's words echoed through the classroom, Janet felt a familiar sense of dread wash over her. She knew this moment was coming, the inevitable pairing with a partner, and the thought of having to interact with someone, let alone a new student, filled her with a debilitating anxiety.

Slowly, Liam made his way towards her desk, and Janet could feel her shoulders instinctively hunch, a futile attempt to make herself smaller and less noticeable. She braced herself for the familiar looks of disappointment or disgust, the silent judgments that had become a constant in her life.

But as Liam approached, his expression remained warm and welcoming, a genuine smile gracing his features. The unexpected kindness in his gaze caught Janet off guard, shattering the preconceptions she had so carefully constructed over the years.

"Hi, Janet," Liam said, his voice soft and reassuring. "I'm really looking forward to working with you on this project."

Janet felt her mouth go dry, the words catching in her throat as she struggled to formulate a response. She risked a quick glance in his direction, only to quickly avert her gaze, unable to maintain eye contact.

"I-I, um, yeah, okay," she managed to mumble, her fingers fidgeting nervously with the hem of her sweater.

The familiar sensation of panic began to rise within her, but there was something about Liam's demeanor, his lack of judgment, that stirred a tiny spark of hope within Janet's heart. She couldn't remember the last time a peer had greeted her with such genuine warmth, and the unfamiliar feeling left her feeling both comforted and deeply unsettled.

As Liam settled into the seat beside her, Janet found herself torn between the instinct to retreat into the safety of her own thoughts and the curious desire to learn more about this new classmate who seemed to see her in a way no one else had before. As Liam began to discuss the details of the upcoming project, she found herself struggling to contribute. Her mind raced with a thousand thoughts, each one more self-deprecating than the last, and the words she longed to say seemed to catch in her throat, refusing to be voiced.

Liam, sensing her discomfort, gently guided the conversation, asking open-ended questions and showing a genuine interest in Janet's ideas. His patient demeanor and lack of judgment slowly began to chip away at the walls she had so carefully constructed, and Janet found herself tentatively opening up.

"What do you think would be a good approach for this project?" Liam asked. His hazel eyes filled with a warmth that Janet had rarely encountered from her peers.

Janet felt her heart racing, the familiar sensation of panic threatening to overwhelm her. She knew the answer, had even formulated a plan in her mind, but the fear of saying the wrong thing, of being ridiculed or dismissed, held her back.

"I-I'm not sure," she stammered, her gaze fixed firmly on the surface of her desk. "Maybe we could, um, focus on the historical context?"

Liam nodded, a small smile playing on his lips. "That's a great idea. I was thinking the same thing. Why don't you tell me more about what you had in mind?"

Encouraged by his receptive response, Janet began to speak, her voice trembling at first, but gradually growing stronger as Liam listened intently, offering thoughtful suggestions and building upon her ideas.

With each passing moment, Janet was surprised by the ease with which she was able to converse with Liam. There was no judgment, no dismissive eye rolls or snide comments, just a genuine interest and a willingness to engage that she had rarely experienced with her peers.

As the class period drew to a close, Janet found herself almost reluctant to part ways, a foreign feeling of comfort and acceptance settling over her. She had spent the better part of the hour in Liam's company, and for once, the overwhelming self-consciousness that typically consumed her had taken a backseat to the unexpected connection they were beginning to forge. As the final bell of the class period rang, Janet braced herself for the inevitable. She fully expected Liam to rush off, eager to be free of her company and the burden of having to interact with someone as socially awkward and insecure as herself.

But to her surprise, Liam turned to her, a warm smile playing on his lips. "Hey, Janet, I was thinking we could meet up in the library after school to continue working on the project. What do you think?"

Janet felt her heart skip a beat, the unexpected invitation catching her off guard. A part of her wanted to retreat, to politely decline and retreat to the safety of her own solitary existence. The familiar voice of self-doubt whispered that it was only a matter of time before Liam realized his mistake, that he would inevitably grow tired of her timid nature and shy away.

Yet, there was a tiny spark of hope ignited by Liam's kindness, a glimmer of possibility that perhaps, just perhaps, she could find a genuine connection with this new classmate who seemed to see her in a way no one else had before.

Swallowing hard, Janet mustered a response, her voice barely above a whisper. "Um, yeah, okay. I-I can do that."

Liam's smile widened, and Janet couldn't help but feel a flutter of something akin to excitement in the pit of her stomach. "Great, I'll meet you in the library around 3:30, then. I'm looking forward to it."

As Liam gathered his things and made his way out of the classroom, Janet found herself rooted to the spot, her mind racing with a whirlwind of emotions. The familiar sense of dread and trepidation still lingered, but it was now tempered by a glimmer of hope, a tiny seed that had been planted by Liam's unexpected kindness.

Steeling herself, Janet took a deep breath and followed suit, her steps a little lighter as she made her way towards the library, her heart pounding with a mixture of anticipation and uncertainty. Janet arrived at the library early, her eyes scanning the rows of shelves and quiet study nooks, searching for the most secluded spot she could find. Spotting an isolated table tucked away in the far corner, she quickly claimed the solitary seat, her fingers gripping the worn strap of her backpack as she settled in.

This was her safe haven, a place where she could retreat from the prying eyes and judgmental stares of her peers. Here, in the quiet sanctuary of the library, Janet felt a sense of peace wash over her, if only for a fleeting moment.

As the minutes ticked by, Janet's gaze remained fixed on the tabletop, her mind a whirlwind of anxious thoughts. She half-expected Liam to never show, that he would have second thoughts about their plans and leave her alone in her solitary corner.

But just as the familiar dread began to settle in, Liam's familiar figure appeared, a warm smile on his face as he approached the table. Janet felt her heart skip a beat, the unexpected warmth of his presence catching her off guard.

"Hey, Janet, he greeted her, his voice soft and reassuring. I hope I didn't keep you waiting too long."

Janet shook her head, her voice barely above a whisper. "No, it's fine. I just got here."

Liam nodded, settling into the chair across from her. As he began to unpack his materials, Janet couldn't help but notice the way his easy-going nature seemed to permeate the isolated space, chasing away the lingering sense of unease that had previously consumed her.

Without a word, they fell into a comfortable rhythm, their discussion of the project flowing with a natural ease that Janet had rarely experienced with her peers. Liam's patient questions and genuine interest in her ideas gradually coaxed her out of her shell, and she started slowly to relax, the familiar weight of self-consciousness lifting from her shoulders.

In that moment, the library felt like a sanctuary, a place where Janet could be herself without the fear of judgment or ridicule. Liam's presence had brought an unexpected warmth to their secluded spot, and as they worked side by side, Janet felt a sense of belonging that she had long since forgotten.

The time seemed to slip away, and Janet was surprised to find herself engaged in the task at hand, her initial trepidation replaced by a newfound focus and sense of purpose. Liam's easy-going nature had created a comfortable atmosphere, one that Janet had never before. As their study session progressed, Liam suddenly paused, his gaze drifting towards the window for a moment before returning to Janet. "I, um, I actually know how it feels to be the new kid, you know?" he said, his voice tinged with a hint of vulnerability.

Janet felt her breath catch in her throat, surprised by Liam's unexpected admission. She had assumed that he, like so many of her other classmates, had always felt at home in their small town, seamlessly navigating the social landscape with a confidence that she could only dream of.

But as Liam shared a personal story about feeling out of place at his previous school, Janet felt a connection forming, a sense of kinship.

Liam's words were hesitant at first, but as he continued, his voice grew stronger, and Janet was drawn in by his honesty and openness. He spoke of the challenges he had faced, the loneliness he had felt, and the determination he had summoned to find his place in a new environment.

The vulnerability in Liam's expression caught Janet off guard, and for a moment, she felt a compulsion to reach out, to offer some form of comfort or reassurance. But the familiar weight of her own insecurities held her back, a lifetime of learned self-preservation instincts keeping her firmly rooted in her seat.

Yet, as Liam's story unfolded, Janet slowly lowered her guard, her own struggles and fears bubbling to the surface. Tentatively, she began to share a bit about her own experiences, her voice trembling at first, but gradually growing stronger as Liam listened without judgment.

She spoke of the relentless teasing from her brothers, the constant feeling of not belonging, and the overwhelming sense of self-consciousness that had become her constant companion. Liam's gaze remained steady, his eyes filled with empathy and understanding, and Janet felt a weight lifting from her shoulders, the burden of her secrets finally finding a safe harbor.

In that moment, Janet felt a connection forming, a shared understanding that transcended the boundaries of their newfound acquaintance. Liam's vulnerability had opened the door, and Janet, against all odds, had found the courage to step through, her heart swelling with a sense of hope that she had long since thought lost. As the afternoon light began to fade, Janet and Liam began to pack up their materials, signaling the end of their study session. As Janet gathered her books and papers, she couldn't help but notice how the time had seemed to slip away, a stark contrast to the constant self-consciousness that typically consumed her.

For hours, she had been in Liam's company, and yet, the familiar worries about her appearance or saying the wrong thing had taken a backseat to the unexpected ease of their conversation. It was a foreign feeling, one that left her both comforted and unsettled, unsure of how to reconcile this newfound sense of belonging with the lifelong insecurities that had become her constant companion.

As she tucked her last notebook into her backpack, a small smile played on Janet's lips, a fleeting expression of contentment that she had rarely allowed herself to indulge in. But just as quickly as it had appeared, she caught herself, the familiar weight of self-consciousness rushing back to the forefront of her mind.

However, Liam's keen eyes had not missed the momentary shift in Janet's demeanor, and he turned to her, a warm smile on his face. "It's nice to see you smile," he said, his voice soft and genuine.

Janet felt her cheeks flush with a sudden heat, and she stammered a response, her gaze quickly darting away. "I-I, um, thank you. I should, uh, get going."

Liam nodded, his expression understanding, and Janet couldn't help but feel a twinge of gratitude for his patience and lack of judgment. As she made her way towards the library exit, she couldn't shake the lingering sense of hope that had taken root within her, a fragile but persistent feeling that perhaps, just perhaps, she had found a kindred spirit in this unexpected new classmate. As Janet made her way home, her mind was a whirlwind of conflicting emotions. The afternoon she had just spent with Liam replayed in her mind, a kaleidoscope of sensations and experiences that left her feeling both hopeful and deeply unsettled.

The familiar weight of self-doubt and insecurity still lingered, a constant companion that had become a part of her very being. A part of her whispered that this newfound connection, this unexpected friendship, was too good to be true – that it was only a matter of time before Liam realized his mistake and abandoned her, just like so many others had before.

But there was a glimmer of hope, a tiny spark that had been ignited by Liam's kindness and genuine interest. Janet couldn't remember the last time a peer had shown her such warmth and understanding, and the thought of having the possibility of a true friendship filled her with a sense of wonder and anxiousness.

She replayed their conversation in her mind, the way Liam had shared his own struggles with feeling out of place, and how his vulnerability had opened the door for her to cautiously share her own burdens. The connection they had forged, however fleeting, felt like a lifeline in the endless sea of judgment and rejection that had become her daily reality.

As Janet's steps carried her closer to the familiar sight of her home, the weight of her doubts and fears threatened to overwhelm her. The prospect of having to face her brothers' relentless taunts and her parents' apparent indifference only served to heighten the turmoil within her.

Yet, for once, Janet allowed herself to hold onto that glimmer of optimism, a tiny flame that flickered and danced in the face of the overwhelming darkness. She knew the path ahead would not be an easy one, that the road to self-acceptance and genuine connection was paved with obstacles and challenges.

But as she replayed Liam's kind smile and the warmth of his gaze, Janet felt a sense of determination take root within her. Perhaps, just perhaps, this new classmate could be the catalyst she needed to finally find the courage to confront her demons and embrace the fullness of her own identity.

With a deep breath, Janet steeled herself for the inevitable confrontation that awaited her at home, her heart still fluttering with a mixture of hope and fear as she considered the possibilities that the future might hold.

STEPPING OUT OF THE SHADOWS

Janet entered the familiar classroom, her fingers gripping the worn strap of her backpack as she scanned the sea of faces. The familiar hum of chatter and laughter filled the air, a stark contrast to the turmoil churning within her.

As her eyes landed on Liam, a flicker of hope ignited in her chest. The new student's kind smile from across the room gave her a small boost of confidence, shattering the overwhelming sense of dread that typically consumed her.

Sinking into her usual seat, Janet found herself more aware of her surroundings than she had been in years. She couldn't help but steal glances at her classmates, observing their interactions with a newfound curiosity. For the first time, she allowed herself to consider the possibility of participating in the lesson, her mind racing with a thousand anxious thoughts.

The teacher's voice rang out, commanding the class's attention, and Janet felt her heart skip a beat. She braced herself, fully expecting the familiar wave of self-consciousness to wash over her, but to her surprise, a flicker of courage began to stir within her.

As the lesson unfolded, she found herself drawn in, her gaze shifting between the teacher and her peers. She noted the way they engaged with the material, their expressions ranging from boredom to genuine interest. And for once, Janet didn't immediately dismiss the idea of contributing, of allowing her own voice to be heard.

The familiar instinct to fade into the background still lingered, a lifetime of learned self-preservation instincts holding her back. But the memory of Liam's encouraging smile, the warmth of his genuine interest, gave her a small glimmer of hope.

Perhaps, just perhaps, this time would be different. Maybe, with Liam's support, she could find the courage to step out of the shadows and let her voice be heard. As the class divided into small groups for a collaborative activity, Janet felt the familiar instinct to fade into the background. Her gaze darted around the room, searching for an opportunity to slip away unnoticed, to avoid the inevitable discomfort of having to interact with her peers.

But then, a memory of Liam's encouraging smile flashed in her mind, and she felt a surge of unexpected courage. Taking a deep breath, she steeled herself and slowly raised her hand, her heart pounding in her chest.

The teacher, visibly surprised, turned to her with a warm smile. "Janet, do you have an idea to share with the group?"

All eyes in the room shifted towards her, and she experienced the familiar rush of self-consciousness wash over her. Her mouth felt dry, and her fingers trembled as she began to speak.

"I, um, I was thinking we could focus on the historical context of the topic," she said, her voice wavering at first. "That way, we could provide a more well-rounded understanding of the subject matter."

As the words left her lips, Janet braced herself for the inevitable dismissal or ridicule. But to her surprise, her classmates turned to listen, their expressions ranging from curiosity to mild approval.

The teacher nodded, her eyes filled with a warmth that she had rarely encountered. "That's an excellent idea, Janet. Why don't you elaborate on that for us?"

Encouraged by the teacher's response, Janet found her voice steadying, the initial tremor giving way to a newfound sense of confidence. She spoke of the importance of understanding the historical factors that had shaped the topic, drawing connections and offering insights that seemed to resonate with her peers.

As she finished, Janet risked a glance around the room, and to her astonishment, she was met with nods of approval and even a few small smiles. The familiar weight of self-consciousness that had so often held her back seemed to have lifted, replaced by a growing sense of pride and accomplishment.

In that moment, she felt a shift within her, a small but significant crack in the armor of insecurity that had long defined her. Liam's belief in her, his constant words of encouragement, had given her the courage to step out of the shadows and let her voice be heard, and the experience left her feeling both exhilarated and deeply unsettled. As the lunch bell rang, Janet felt inclined to her usual instinct to retreat to the solitary safety of her favorite corner of the cafeteria and the unexpected desire to seek out Liam's company.

The memory of his kind smile and genuine interest in her ideas still lingered, and she couldn't help but feel a flutter of hope at the prospect of continuing their budding friendship. Yet, the familiar weight of self-consciousness and the fear of rejection held her back, whispering that she was unworthy of such kindness.

Steeling herself, Janet scanned the crowded cafeteria, her gaze finally landing on Liam's familiar figure. To her surprise, he caught her eye and waved her over, a warm smile gracing his features.

Before she could even process the invitation, a sudden movement in her peripheral vision caught her attention. Her brothers, their faces twisted in sneers, approached, and Janet felt her heart sink.

"Well, if it isn't our little piglet," one of them jeered, his voice dripping with disdain. "Looks like you've finally found someone desperate enough to hang out with you."

She froze, the familiar rush of shame and embarrassment washing over her. She felt the weight of her brothers' cruel words, the sting of their taunts cutting deeper than ever before. In that moment, she wanted nothing more than to disappear, to escape the humiliation of their public ridicule.

But just as the familiar panic began to rise within her, Liam's voice cut through the haze, firm and un wavering.

"That's enough," he said, his hazel eyes narrowing with a quiet intensity. "Janet is my friend, and I won't stand by while you treat her that way."

Janet's brothers, taken aback by Liam's unexpected defense, fell silent, their sneers momentarily replaced by expressions of shock and disbelief.

Liam continued, his words laced with a quiet conviction. "Janet is a kind, intelligent person, and she deserves to be treated with respect. I suggest you think twice before you open your mouths to insult her again."

The cafeteria fell silent, all eyes turning towards the confrontation unfolding before them. Her heart pounding in her chest, felt a surge of gratitude and disbelief wash over her. Liam, this unexpected friend, had stood up for her in a way no one else had before, and the realization left her both comforted and deeply unsettled.

As her brothers, rendered momentarily speechless, turned and retreated, Janet remained rooted to the spot, her gaze locked with Liam's. In that moment, she felt a connection forming, a shared understanding that transcended the boundaries of their newfound acquaintance.

The afternoon, at English class, the familiar scent of books and the hush of quiet contemplation enveloped her. As the teacher began to discuss the day's lesson on poetry, she felt a surprising stirring within her.

For years, she had sat silently in this very room, her gaze fixed on the pages before her, carefully avoiding any opportunity to draw attention to herself. The mere thought of reading aloud, of allowing her voice to be heard, had always filled her with a crippling sense of dread.

But today, something was different. The memory of Liam's constant support, his willingness to stand up for her in the face of her brothers' cruelty, had ignited a small flame of courage within her. And as the teacher asked for volunteers to read the poem they had been studying, Janet felt a surge of unexpected determination.

Slowly, almost against her better judgment, she raised her hand, her heart pounding in her chest. The teacher, visibly surprised, called on her, and Janet felt the weight of her classmates' curious gazes upon her.

Taking a deep breath, she began to read, her voice trembling at first. But as the words flowed from her lips, she became lost in the rhythm and cadence of the poem, her initial hesitation giving way to a quiet intensity.

With each line, Janet's voice grew stronger, her confidence building as she immersed herself in the vivid imagery and emotive language. The familiar self-consciousness that had so often held her back seemed to fade into the background, replaced by a sense of focus and purpose.

As she finished, Janet slowly lifted her gaze, her eyes meeting those of her classmates and teacher. To her surprise, she was met not with the dismissive eye rolls or snide comments she had come to expect, but with expressions of genuine interest and even a hint of respect.

The teacher offered her a warm smile, her words of praise filling her with a sense of pride and accomplishment that she had rarely experienced. In that moment, she felt a shift within her, a small but significant crack in the armor of insecurity that had long defined her.

Liam's support and belief in her had given her the courage to step out of the shadows and let her voice be heard. And as she sat there, basking in the newfound respect of her peers, she couldn't help but feel a glimmer of hope that perhaps, just perhaps, she was capable of so much more than she had ever dared to imagine. As the final bell of the day rang, Janet gathered her belongings and made her way out of the school, the weight of her backpack a comforting anchor in the swirl of emotions coursing through her.

The events of the day replayed in her mind, a kaleidoscope of experiences that left her feeling both exhilarated and deeply unsettled. She had stepped out of the shadows, raising her hand to contribute in class, reading a poem aloud with confidence, and with Liam's support by standing up to her brothers' cruel taunts.

It was a far cry from the timid, self-conscious girl she had become accustomed to being, and the realization left her feeling a mix of pride and disbelief. Had she truly found the courage to challenge the ingrained insecurities that had long defined her?

As Janet walked the familiar path towards home, her steps slowed as she passed the local community theater. The sounds of laughter and music drifted out through the open doors, and she paused, drawn to the energy and vibrancy that emanated from the building.

For a moment, she allowed her mind to wander, imagining herself on that stage, her voice strong and confident as she embodied a character, fully expressing the depth of her emotions. The thought both thrilled and terrified her, a tantalizing possibility that seemed to both beckon and taunt her.

Janet had always loved the theater, the way the actors could so effortlessly transport the audience to another world, evoking a range of emotions with their words and movements. But the idea of stepping into the spotlight, of potentially facing the judgment and scrutiny of an audience, had always filled her with a crippling sense of dread.

Yet, as she stood there, the sounds of the theater washing over her, she couldn't help but feel a stirring of curiosity and wonder. Liam's belief in her had ignited a small flame of courage within her, and she wondered if perhaps, just perhaps, she could muster the strength to step out of the shadows and onto that stage.

The thought both exhilarated and terrified her, a dizzying mix of emotions that left her feeling both hopeful and deeply unsettled. But as she continued on her way home, Janet couldn't shake the lingering sense of possibility, the tantalizing idea that she might one day find the courage to embrace her dreams and let her voice be heard. As she stepped through the front door, the familiar sounds of her brothers' banter filled the air, a constant backdrop to the life she had grown accustomed to. But as their taunting voices reached her ears, she was surprised to find that their words no longer stung with the same intensity.

The events of the day had left an indelible mark on her, chipping away at the armor of insecurity that had long shielded her from the cruel realities of her home life. Liam's relentless support, the respect from her classmates, and the small acts of courage she had mustered: all of these experiences had coalesced into a change within her, a subtle but significant change that she could feel taking root.

Navigating the familiar hallway of her home, Janet caught a glimpse of herself in the hallway mirror, and for the first time in years, she didn't immediately look away in disgust like before. Instead, she paused, her gaze locking with her own reflection, she found herself searching for the glimmer of strength and resilience that had manifested itself earlier in the day.

The girl staring back at her was not the same timid, self-conscious individual she had grown accustomed to seeing. There was a newfound spark in her eyes, a quiet determination that had been absent for so long. And as Janet held her own gaze, she felt a surge of pride and disbelief wash over her.

She had faced her fears, had found the courage to step out of the shadows and let her voice be heard. The memory of her classmates' approving nods, the warmth in the teacher's eyes, and Liam's support – all of these moments were chipping away the deep-seated insecurities that had long defined her.

In that brief moment, she saw a glimpse of the person she could become, a young woman unafraid to embrace her own unique identity and let it shine. The thought was both exhilarating and terrifying, a dizzying mix of emotions that left her feeling both hopeful and deeply unsettled.

As her brothers' taunts continued to echo in the background, she found that their words no longer held the same power over her. The familiar sting of shame and embarrassment had been dulled, replaced by a growing sense of self-acceptance and resilience.

She knew the road ahead would not be an easy one, that the journey to fully embracing her own worth and potential would be paved with challenges and obstacles. But in that moment, as she held her own gaze in the mirror, she felt a quiet determination take root within her.

She was no longer the same girl who had walked through those doors earlier that day. Something had shifted, a small but significant change that had the power to transform her entire world. And as she turned away from the mirror, she couldn't help but feel a glimmer of hope that perhaps, just perhaps, this was only the beginning.

As the evening shadows crept across Janet's bedroom, still hunched over her desk, her brow furrowed in concentration as she worked through her homework assignments. The familiar routine of studying and completing her schoolwork had always provided a sense of comfort and structure, a welcome respite from the turmoil that often consumed her thoughts. But tonight, something was different. And as she sat there, Janet couldn't help but feel a lingering sense of pride and accomplishment.

Suddenly, the soft chime of her phone broke the stillness of the room, and Janet felt her heart skip a beat. Glancing down at the screen, she was surprised to see a message from Liam, her new classmate and unexpected ally.

"Hey, Janet," the message read, "I just wanted to say how impressed I was with your contributions in class today. You really showed your smarts, and I'm proud of you for stepping up like that. Keep it up!"

Janet felt a warm glow of accomplishment wash over her, the simple words of praise from Liam filling her with a sense of validation she had rarely experienced. For so long, she had been conditioned to dismiss any positive feedback, to automatically assume that she was unworthy of such recognition.

But as she stared at the message, her fingers hovering over the keyboard, she paused. The familiar urge to respond with a self-deprecating quip, to downplay her own achievements, bubbled to the surface. It was a knee-jerk reaction, a lifetime of learned behavior that had become second nature.

Yet, in that moment, something shifted within her. The memory of the day's events, the small acts of courage she had mustered, the newfound respect she had garnered from her peers – all of these experiences had coalesced into a growing sense of self-worth and determination.

Slowly, Janet deleted the self-deprecating response she had begun to type, and instead, she crafted a genuine message of gratitude.

"Thank you, Liam," she typed, her fingers trembling slightly. "Your encouragement means a lot to me."

As she pressed send, Janet felt a surge of pride and accomplishment wash over her. It was a small act, a simple response to a kind message, but in that moment, it felt like a significant victory. She had chosen to embrace her own worth, to acknowledge the progress she had made, rather than retreating into the familiar patterns of self-doubt and insecurity.

The realization left Janet feeling both exhilarated and deeply unsettled. She knew that the journey ahead would not be an easy one, that the road to fully embracing her own identity would be paved with challenges and obstacles. But in that moment, as she set aside her homework and allowed herself to bask in the warmth of Liam's message, she felt a glimmer of hope that perhaps, just perhaps, she was finally beginning to find her voice. As the evening drew to a close, Janet sat at her desk, her journal still open before her. The familiar leather-bound book had long been her constant companion, a safe haven where she could pour out the thoughts and emotions she struggled to express in her everyday life.

Tonight, however, the pages seemed to beckon to her in a different way. The events of the day had left an indelible mark on her, a series of small yet significant moments that had chipped away at the deep-seated insecurities that had so often defined her.

With a deep breath, Janet began to write, her pen gliding across the crisp pages as she poured out her thoughts and reflections. She acknowledged the lingering fear and self-doubt that still lurked within her, the familiar voices of insecurity that whispered in the back of her mind.

But interwoven with those doubts, she also recognized the small seeds of confidence that had begun to take root. The memory of her contributions in class, the warmth in her teacher's eyes, and the support of Liam – all of these experiences had left an indelible mark on her, slowly chipping away at the armor of self-consciousness that had long shielded her from the world.

As she wrote, Janet felt a sense of vulnerability and raw honesty that she had rarely allowed herself to embrace. The words flowed freely, a cathartic release of the emotions she had long suppressed, and with each line, she could feel the weight of her burdens beginning to lift.

Yet, even as she acknowledged the progress she had made, Janet knew that the road to fully embracing her own worth and potential was paved with challenges and obstacles, and that the familiar specter of self-doubt still lingered, a constant companion that refused to be silenced.

But as she closed the journal and set it aside, she made a quiet promise to herself. She would nurture those small seeds of confidence, no matter how daunting the task might seem. She would continue to push past her fears, to find the courage to step out of the shadows and let her voice be heard.

It would not be an easy path, but the experiences of the day had shown her that she was capable of more than she had ever dared to imagine, and with Liam by her side and her own growing sense of self-worth, she knew that she had the strength to overcome the obstacles that lay ahead.

As she settled into bed, the familiar weight of exhaustion settling over her, Janet allowed herself a small smile. Tomorrow would bring new challenges, new opportunities to confront her fears and embrace her own unique identity. But for now, she would savor the progress she had made, the small victories that had begun to chip away at the walls of insecurity that had long defined her.

With a deep breath, Janet closed her eyes, her mind already whirring with the possibilities that the future might hold.

A CHANCE ENCOUNTER

The familiar streets of Janet's small town blurred together as she walked home from school, her mind consumed by the events of the day. The newfound confidence she had discovered in the classroom still lingered, a flickering flame that both thrilled and unsettled her.

As she turned the corner, her usual route home, Janet felt a tug of unease. The familiar sights and sounds of her neighborhood had become a well-worn path, a safe haven from the judgment and ridicule she so often faced. But today, something felt different.

Slowing her pace, Janet allowed her gaze to wander, taking in the details of her surroundings with a newfound awareness. The familiar storefronts and weathered sidewalks gave way to an unexpected sight – the local community theater, its doors flung open, the sounds of laughter and music spilling out into the street.

Janet paused, her steps faltering as she found herself drawn to the energy and vibrancy emanating from the building. For as long as she could remember, she had passed this place countless times, her eyes always downcast, her mind focused on the familiar path home. But today, something compelled her to linger, to allow her curiosity to override the cautious instincts that had long governed her.

As she drew closer, the sounds of the theater washed over her, a symphony of voices, music, and the occasional burst of applause. Janet felt a flutter of wonder in her chest, a stirring of emotions she had long suppressed. The theater had always held a certain allure for her, a place where she could lose herself in the magic of story-telling and self-expression.

Yet, the very idea of stepping into that world, of potentially facing the scrutiny and judgment of an audience, had filled her with a crippling sense of dread. Janet had spent so much of her life shrinking away from the spotlight, desperate to avoid the cruel taunts and dismissive glances of her peers.

But today, as she stood before the open doors of the theater, some-thing felt different. All of these experiences had chipped away at the armor of insecurity that had long defined her.

Tentatively, Janet inched closer, her gaze drawn to the flurry of activity within. She watched, transfixed, as a group of people moved about the stage, their expressions filled with a palpable energy and passion. And in that moment, she couldn't help but wonder – what would it feel like to be up there, to let her voice be heard, to shed the constraints of her own self-doubt and truly embrace the freedom of self-expression?

The thought both thrilled and terrified her, a dizzying mix of emotions that left her feeling both hopeful and deeply unsettled. But as the sounds of joy and laughter continued to beckon, she took a deep breath, her fingers tightening around the strap of her backpack as she steeled her resolve.

Curiosity had always been a double-edged sword for Janet, a temptation that both drew her in and filled her with a crippling sense of fear. But in this moment, as she stood before the open doors of the community theater, she felt a shift within her – a small but significant crack in the armor of insecurity that had long defined her.

With a steadying breath, Janet took a step forward, her heart pounding in her chest as she crossed the threshold, her world forever changed.

Drawn by the sounds of the theater, she was attracted to a large window, peering inside with a mixture of wonder and trepidation. Through the glass, she could see a group of people gathered on the dimly lit stage, their movements fluid and expressive as they rehearsed.

Janet's gaze was immediately drawn to a young woman center stage, her voice filling the space with a raw, emotive intensity. She watched, transfixed, as the actress delivered a monologue, her words and gestures conveying a depth of feeling that Janet had rarely witnessed.

For a moment, she felt herself transported, her own insecurities and fears momentarily forgotten as she became lost in the performance. The actress on stage seemed to move with a confidence and freedom that Janet could scarcely imagine, her every word and movement imbued with a captivating power.

Unconsciously, Janet felt herself leaning closer, her breath catching in her throat as she imagined herself in that very same spotlight. The thought both thrilled and terrified her, a dizzying mix of emotions that left her feeling both exhilarated and deeply unsettled.

To be free from the constraints of her own self-doubt, to shed the weight of the insecurities that had long defined her – the idea was both intoxicating and deeply unsettling. Janet had spent so much of her life shrinking away from the judgment of others, hiding behind a carefully constructed facade of timidity and self-consciousness.

But in that moment, as she watched the actress command the stage with such raw, unapologetic passion, Janet felt a stirring of longing deep within her. To be seen, to be heard, to truly express the depth of her own emotions – it was a tantalizing possibility that both beckoned and taunted her.

The voices of her brothers, the dismissive glances of her classmates – they all echoed in her mind, a constant reminder of the judgment and ridicule that had shaped her reality. And yet, as Janet continued to observe the rehearsal, she couldn't help but feel a glimmer of hope that perhaps, just perhaps, there was another path, a world where she could find the courage to step out of the shadows and into the light.

The thought was both exhilarating and deeply unsettling, a dizzying mix of emotions that left Janet feeling both hopeful and utterly terrified. But as she stood there, her gaze transfixed by the performers on stage, she knew that something within her had shifted – another small but significant crack in the armor of insecurity that had long defined her. As Janet stood transfixed, watching the rehearsal unfold before her, the sound of the theater's door creaking open startled her, pulling her from her reverie. Instinctively, she tensed, her heart racing as she prepared to flee, the familiar panic rising within her.

But then, a warm, friendly voice called out, and Janet's gaze shifted to a woman in her forties, her expression open and inviting. "Hello there," the woman said, her smile radiating a genuine warmth that caught Janet off guard. "I couldn't help but notice you standing out here. Would you like to come inside and take a look around?"

For a moment, Janet felt frozen, her mind racing with a thousand conflicting thoughts. Every fiber of her being urged her to turn and run, to retreat back to the safety of the familiar streets and the comfort of her own solitude. The idea of stepping into that theater, of potentially facing the scrutiny and judgment of strangers, filled her with a crippling sense of dread.

And yet, as Janet met the woman's kind gaze, she felt a flicker of something unexpected – a small, fragile glimmer of curiosity that refused to be extinguished. There was something about the woman's warm smile, the genuine invitation in her voice, that seemed to cut through the haze of Janet's own self-doubt and insecurity.

Caught in the throes of an internal struggle, she felt her fingers tighten around the strap of her backpack, her knuckles turning white as she fought to steady her racing heart. The temptation to flee, to retreat back to the safety of the known, was nearly over-whelming. But as she stood there, the sounds of the rehearsal still drifting out through the open door, Janet couldn't shake the lingering sense of possibility that had taken root within her.

With a deep, steadying breath, Janet felt a shift within her, a small but significant crack in her armor of insecurity. Summoning every ounce of courage she could muster, she took a step forward, her gaze meeting the woman's with a newfound determination.

"I-I'd like that," Janet heard herself say, her voice barely above a whisper. But as the words left her lips, she felt a surge of pride and accomplishment, a testament to the small victories she had already claimed that day.

Without another moment's hesitation, Janet crossed the thresh-old, her heart pounding in her chest as she stepped into the vibrant world of the community theater, her life forever changed. As Janet stepped across the threshold, the energy and passion of the community theater immediately enveloped her, leaving her both exhilarated and deeply unsettled. The bustling activity, the lively chatter, and the palpable sense of creativity that permeated the space were a stark contrast to the quiet solitude she had grown so accustomed to.

Glancing around, Janet's gaze was drawn to the woman who had welcomed her inside, her warm smile and friendly demeanor putting her slightly at ease. "Welcome to our little corner of the world," the woman said, her voice rich and inviting. "I'm Maria, the director. We're just in the middle of rehearsals for our upcoming production."

Janet felt her heart flutter with a mix of excitement and trepidation as Maria continued, explaining the details of the upcoming show and the vibrant community of actors and crew members who brought it to life. For as long as she could remember, the theater had held a certain allure for Janet, a world of self-expression and storytelling that had always seemed just out of reach.

"I've always been interested in theater," Janet confessed, the words tumbling from her lips before she could stop them. "But I've never had the courage to actually pursue it."

As the admission left her, Janet felt a familiar wave of self-consciousness wash over her, the urge to shrink back and disappear nearly overwhelming. But to her surprise, Maria's eyes lit up, a spark of genuine excitement and encouragement shining through.

"Well, you've certainly come to the right place, then," Maria replied, her tone warm and welcoming. "We're always looking for new talent, and I can see the spark in you. Have you ever considered auditioning for one of our shows?"

The question hung in the air, a tantalizing possibility that both thrilled and terrified Janet. To step onto that stage, to shed the constraints of her own insecurities and truly embrace the freedom of self-expression — the idea was both exhilarating and deeply unsettling.

Janet felt her fingers tighten around the strap of her backpack, her mind racing with a thousand conflicting thoughts. The voices of her brothers, the dismissive glances of her classmates — they all echoed in her head, a constant reminder of the judgment and ridicule that had shaped her reality.

And yet, as she stood there, surrounded by the energy and passion of the theater, Janet couldn't help but feel a glimmer of hope. Perhaps, in this vibrant and accepting community, she could find the courage to take that first step, to shed the constraints of her own self-doubt and embrace the possibility that lay before her.

Swallowing hard, she met Maria's gaze, a newfound determination flickering in her eyes. "I...I think I'd like that," she said, her voice steadier than she had expected. "I'd love to audition." With Maria's encouragement still ringing in her ears, she was drawn deeper into the world of the community theater, her gaze darting around the bustling space as she took in the energy and passion that permeated every corner.

As she observed the ongoing rehearsal, Janet was struck by the supportive atmosphere that surrounded the cast and crew. She watched, transfixed, as one of the actors stumbled over his lines, his brow furrowed in concentration as he struggled to regain his footing.

Instinctively, Janet braced herself, expecting to witness the familiar scene of ridicule and judgment that had so often played out in her own life. But to her surprise, the actor's castmates immediately sprang into action, offering words of encouragement and helpful tips to guide him through the challenging moment.

The contrast was jarring, a stark difference from the cruel taunts and dismissive glances that Janet had grown accustomed to enduring, both at school and within the confines of her own home. As she watched the supportive exchange unfold before her, a sense of longing and possibility began to take root within her.

This was a world unlike anything she had ever known, a community where the pursuit of self-expression and creativity was celebrated, rather than mocked. The actors moved with a confidence and freedom that she could scarcely imagine, their every word and gesture imbued with a raw, unapologetic passion.

And in that moment, as Janet observed the rehearsal, she couldn't help but wonder – what would it feel like to be up there, to shed the constraints of her own self-doubt and truly embrace the power of her own voice? The thought both thrilled and terrified her, a dizzying mix of emotions that left her feeling both hopeful and deeply unsettled.

For so long, she had been conditioned to shrink away from the spotlight, to avoid drawing any unnecessary attention to herself. The familiar voices of her brothers, the dismissive glances of her classmates – they had all served to reinforce the notion that she was unworthy of being seen or heard, that her own thoughts and feelings were somehow less valuable than those of her peers.

But as she stood there, immersed in the supportive, creative atmosphere of the theater, Janet felt a shift within her. The small cracks in the armor of insecurity that had begun to form were now widening, allowing a glimmer of possibility to seep through.

Perhaps, in this vibrant community, she could find the courage to step out of the shadows and into the light, to embrace the fullness of her own voice and the depth of her own emotions. The thought was both exhilarating and deeply unsettling, but as Janet continued to observe the rehearsal, she knew that something within her had irrevocably changed. As the rehearsal continued, Janet found herself drawn deeper into the vibrant world of the community theater, her gaze darting from one performer to the next as she marveled at the energy and passion that permeated the space.

Suddenly, the rhythm of the rehearsal was interrupted by a break, and Janet watched as the cast and crew scattered, some retreating to the sidelines to grab a quick sip of water, others engaging in animated conversations. And to her surprise, a small group of the younger performers began to make their way towards her, their expressions curious and welcoming.

Janet felt her heart skip a beat as they approached, the familiar instinct to shrink back and disappear nearly overwhelming. But as the young actors drew closer, she was struck by the genuine warmth and openness in their demeanor, a stark contrast to the judgment and ridicule she had grown so accustomed to facing.

Hi there, one of the girls said, her voice lilting with a friendly cadence. We haven't seen you around before. I'm Lily, and this is Ethan and Sophia. Are you new to the theater?

For a moment, Janet felt her tongue tied, the weight of their curious gazes leaving her feeling uncharacteristically self-conscious. But as she met their friendly smiles, she felt a flicker of courage begin to stir within her.

"I-I'm Janet," she managed to say, her voice barely above a whisper. "And yes, this is my first time here. I've always been interested in theater, but I've never really had the chance to pursue it."

The young actors' expressions lit up with genuine interest, and they began to pepper Janet with questions, asking about her interests and experiences. And to her own surprise, she was opening up, her usual guardedness began to soften in the face of their welcoming demeanor.

She spoke of her love for storytelling, her fascination with the way actors could so effortlessly transport an audience to another world. And as she did, she was struck by the genuine attentiveness of her new companions, their eyes shining with a shared passion and understanding.

This was a world unlike anything Janet had ever known, a community where creativity and self-expression were celebrated, rather than mocked. Gone were the familiar taunts and dismissive glances that had so often defined her experiences, replaced by a palpable sense of acceptance and camaraderie.

As the young actors continued to engage with her, Janet felt a weight lifting from her shoulders, the familiar armor of insecurity that had long shielded her started to crack and crumble. In this vibrant, supportive environment, she was opening up, allowing glimpses of her true self to shine through.

And in that moment, as she stood there, surrounded by the warmth and enthusiasm of her new companions, Janet couldn't help but feel a glimmer of hope ignite within her. Perhaps, in this world of theater and storytelling, she could finally find the courage to step out of the shadows and into the light, to embrace the fullness of her own voice and the depth of her own emotions. As the rehearsal began to wind down, Janet was reluctant to leave the vibrant world of the community theater. The energy and passion that had surrounded her, the warmth and acceptance of her new young companions – it was all a far cry from the familiar confines of her daily life.

Suddenly, Maria approached, a warm smile gracing her features as she turned her attention to Janet. "I'm so glad you decided to come in and take a look around," she said, her voice rich with genuine enthusiasm. "We're always looking for new talent, and I can see the spark in you."

With that, Maria reached into the pocket of her jeans, producing a neatly folded flyer and pressing it into Janet's hands. "This is for our upcoming auditions," she explained. "I really think you should consider giving it a try."

Janet felt the weight of the paper in her palm, the crisp edges a tangible representation of the possibility that lay before her. Her mind raced with a whirlwind of conflicting emotions – excitement at the prospect of exploring this new world, and a paralyzing fear of putting herself out there, of potentially facing the judgment and ridicule that had so often defined her experiences.

The voices of her brothers, the dismissive glances of her classmates – they all echoed in her head, a constant reminder of the obstacles she had faced. To step onto that stage, to shed the constraints of her own self-doubt and truly embrace the freedom of self-expression – the idea was both exhilarating and deeply unsettling.

Janet's fingers tightened around the flyer, her knuckles turning white as she grappled with the weight of her own insecurities. What if she wasn't good enough? What if she stumbled over her lines or froze under the scrutiny of an audience? The fear of failure, of further ridicule, was a constant companion, a shadow that had long cast a pall over her dreams and aspirations.

And yet, as Janet stood there, surrounded by the supportive, creative energy of the theater, she couldn't help but feel a glimmer of hope begin to take root within her. This was a world unlike anything she had ever known, a community where the pursuit of self-expression was celebrated, rather than mocked.

Perhaps, in this vibrant and accepting environment, she could finally find the courage to take that first step, to shed the constraints of her own self-doubt and embrace the fullness of her own voice. The thought was both exhilarating and deeply unsettling, a dizzying mix of emotions that left her feeling both hopeful and utterly terrified.

Swallowing hard, Janet carefully tucked the audition flyer into the pocket of her jeans, the weight of the paper a constant reminder of the potential that lay before her. With each step she took towards the exit, the familiar doubts and fears echoed in her mind again, but beneath them, a small, fragile flame of determination had been ignited. As Janet stepped out of the community theater, the weight of the audition flyer in her pocket felt both exhilarating and deeply unsettling. Her mind raced with a whirlwind of possibilities and doubts, the familiar voices of her brothers and classmates echoing in her head.

She could still vividly picture herself on that stage, free from the constraints of her own insecurities, her voice strong and confident as she embodied a character and expressed emotions she had long suppressed. The thought both thrilled and terrified her.

But as Janet walked the familiar path towards home, the mocking laughter of her brothers and the dismissive glances of her peers began to creep back into her consciousness. They would never understand, she knew – how could they, when she had spent so much of her life shrinking away from the spotlight, desperate to avoid their cruel taunts and judgment?

The weight of their ridicule felt heavy, a burden that threatened to extinguish the small, fragile flame of determination that had been ignited within her. She could already hear their voices, the cruel jabs and derisive comments that would surely follow if she dared to pursue her newfound dream.

Yet, as she walked, her fingers instinctively reached for the flyer in her pocket, the crisp edges a tangible reminder of the possibility that lay before her. This was a chance, a glimmer of hope in a world that had long felt devoid of such things. And despite the fear and self-doubt that threatened to consume her, Janet couldn't help but feel a stirring of determination deep within her core.

Slowly, she withdrew the flyer, her gaze sweeping over the details of the upcoming auditions. The words seemed to dance before her eyes, a siren's call that both beckoned and taunted her. To step out of the shadows, to embrace the fullness of her own voice and the depth of her own emotions – the idea was both exhilarating and deeply unsettling.

As she approached the familiar confines of her home, Janet carefully tucked the flyer back into her bag, shielding it from prying eyes. It was a secret treasure, a silent act of defiance against the insecurities that had long defined her. And in that moment, as she crossed the threshold, she felt a quiet resolve begin to take root within her.

She may not be ready to face the judgment of her brothers or the ridicule of her peers, not yet. But the memory of the theater, the warmth and acceptance she had found in the embrace of that vibrant community, had left an indelible mark on her. And deep within her heart, a small, fragile flame of hope had been ignited – a spark that refused to be extinguished, no matter the obstacles that lay ahead.

A SUPPORTIVE FRIENDSHIP

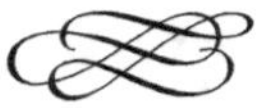

Janet's fingers trembled as she gripped the crinkled theater audition flyer, her heart pounding in her chest. The weight of the paper felt both exhilarating and terrifying at the same time, a tangible representation of the possibility that lay before her – and the fear that threatened to consume her.

Steeling her nerves, Janet scanned the cafeteria, her gaze finally settling on Liam, who was seated at a nearby table, engrossed in a conversation with a group of their classmates. Taking a deep, steadying breath, she began to make her way towards him, her steps tentative and unsure.

As she drew closer, Liam glanced up, his warm, friendly smile immediately putting Janet at ease. There was a genuine kindness in his expression that had a way of cutting through the haze of her own self-doubt, and in that moment, Janet felt a flicker of courage ignite within her.

"Hi, Liam," she said, her voice barely above a whisper. Clutching the audition flyer tightly, she hesitated, second-guessing herself as a familiar wave of insecurity threatened to overwhelm her. But then, Liam's eyes met hers, and she saw a spark of genuine interest and encouragement that gave her the strength to continue.

"I, um..." Janet paused, her gaze dropping to the flyer in her hands. "I found this at the community theater, and I was wondering..." Her voice trailed off, the weight of her own uncertainty causing the words to catch in her throat.

Liam's expression shifted, his brow furrowing with a mixture of curiosity and concern. Reaching across the table, he gently placed his hand on Janet's arm, the simple gesture both steadying and reassuring.

"What is it, Janet?" he asked, his tone soft and inviting. "You can tell me."

Janet felt her heart skip a beat at his touch, the warmth of his hand sending a small thrill through her. Swallowing hard, she lifted the flyer, her trembling fingers revealing the bold text that announced the upcoming auditions for the community theater's latest production.

"I... I want to audition," she whispered, her voice barely audible over the din of the cafeteria. "But I'm so scared, Liam. What if I'm not good enough? What if they laugh at me again?"

The words tumbled out in a rush, a torrent of fears and insecurities that Janet had kept buried for so long. She felt exposed, vulnerable, and yet, in Liam's unwavering gaze, she found a glimmer of understanding and support that she had never experienced before.

Liam's eyes widened with a mix of surprise and excitement, and Janet watched as a smile slowly spread across his face. Reaching out, he gently took the flyer from her hands, his fingers tracing over the details with a palpable sense of enthusiasm.

"Janet, this is amazing!" he exclaimed, his voice brimming with genuine encouragement. "I think you should absolutely go for it. And I'd be honored to help you prepare, if you'd like."

Janet felt her breath catch in her throat, the weight of his words washing over her in a dizzying wave. Help her prepare? The idea was both thrilling and terrifying, a temptation that both beckoned and taunted her.

For so long, she had hidden behind the safety of her own self-doubt, afraid to step out of the shadows and into the spotlight. The memories of her brothers' cruel taunts and the dismissive glances of her peers still haunted her, a constant reminder of the judgment and ridicule that had shaped her reality.

But as Liam's eyes shone with unwavering belief, Janet felt a tiny flame of hope ignite within her. Perhaps, in this moment, she could find the courage to take that first step, to shed the constraints of her own insecurities and embrace the possibility that lay before her.

Swallowing hard, she nodded, her gaze meeting Liam's with a newfound determination. "I'd like that," she whispered, her voice steadier than she had expected. "I'd really like that."

In that instant, Janet felt a shift within her, another small but significant crack in the armor of insecurity that had long defined her. And as Liam's face lit up with excitement, she knew that she had taken the first step on a journey that would forever change the course of her life. The bell rang and they both went back to class.

The final school bell rang, signaling the end of the day, and Janet felt a familiar flutter of nerves in the pit of her stomach. Clutching the theater audition flyer tightly, she scanned the bustling hallway, her gaze finally settling on Liam as he approached with a warm smile.

"Ready to get started?" he asked, his voice brimming with enthusiasm.

Janet nodded, though the tightness in her chest betrayed the anxiety that threatened to consume her. As they made their way to an empty classroom, her mind raced with a thousand conflicting thoughts – what if she wasn't good enough? What if she froze up and embarrassed herself in front of Liam?

The classroom was quiet and serene, a stark contrast to the chaos of the hallways. Liam gestured for Janet to take a seat, then pulled up a chair beside her, his expression open and encouraging.

"Okay, let's take a look at this monologue you've been working on," he said, his tone gentle and reassuring. "Why don't you give it a try, and I'll offer some feedback."

Janet felt her heart pounding in her ears as she unfolded the crumpled pages, her fingers trembling slightly. Clearing her throat, she began to read, her voice barely above a whisper as the words tumbled out.

Almost immediately, she stumbled, her mind going blank as she struggled to remember the next line. Panic began to rise within her, and she felt her cheeks flush with embarrassment.

But then, Liam's hand reached out, gently resting on her arm. "Hey, it's okay," he said, his voice soothing. "Take a deep breath, and let's try that part again."

Janet nodded, forcing herself to inhale deeply. As she exhaled, she felt some of the tension in her shoulders begin to dissipate. Locking eyes with Liam, she took another steadying breath and resumed the monologue, her voice growing stronger with each passing line.

Liam listened intently, offering the occasional nod or encouraging smile. When she reached the end, he clapped his hands together, his expression beaming with pride.

"Janet, that was amazing!" he exclaimed. "Your delivery was so powerful, and I could really feel the emotion behind the words."

Janet felt a flush of warmth spread across her cheeks, a mix of pride and disbelief. For so long, she had been conditioned to doubt her own abilities, to shrink away from any form of praise or recognition. But in this moment, with Liam's unconditional support, she allowed herself to bask in the glow of his encouragement.

"Really?" she asked, her voice barely above a whisper. "You really think I can do this?"

Liam nodded emphatically, his eyes shining with sincerity. "Absolutely," he replied. "And I'm going to be right here, every step of the way, to help you get ready."

As his words sank in, Janet felt a glimmer of hope begin to take root within her. The idea of stepping onto that stage, of shedding the constraints of her own self-doubt and embracing the fullness of her own voice, was both exhilarating and deeply unsettling. But with Liam by her side, guiding her gently and offering his support, she began to envision the possibility of success.

Slowly, tentatively, Janet allowed herself to imagine the thrill of standing in the spotlight, of captivating an audience with the power of her own performance. And in that moment, she felt a shift within her, another small but significant crack in the armor of the insecurity that had defined her for so long.

Janet found herself relaxing more and more as they continued to work through the monologue, with Liam's patient encouragement and practical tips helping to bolster her confidence. Her voice grew stronger, her movements more assured, and with each passing minute, she allowed herself to believe that perhaps, just perhaps, she could do this.

For the first time in her life, she began to envision a future where she wasn't defined by the limitations of her own self-doubt, where she could embrace the fullness of her own voice and the depth of her own emotions. And as she met Liam's gaze, his eyes shining with pride and belief, she knew that she had taken the first steps on a journey that would forever change the course of her life,

As the sun dipped below the horizon, casting long shadows across the quiet suburban streets, Janet slipped quietly into the sanctuary of her family's bathroom. The familiar tile walls and worn linoleum floor offered a sense of solace, a refuge from the prying eyes and taunting voices that so often filled her days.

Closing the door behind her, Janet turned to face the mirror, her gaze settling on her own reflection. For a moment, she simply stood there, her fingers tracing the faint lines of worry that had begun to etch themselves into her brow. The weight of her brothers' relentless bullying and the constant fear of judgment from her peers had taken a toll, leaving her feeling small and insignificant.

But then, her eyes fell upon the crumpled pages of the monologue she had been practicing, and a spark of determination ignited within her. Clearing her throat, she began to whisper the lines, her voice tentative at first, then growing stronger with each passing word.

As she immersed herself in the words, something shifted within Janet. The familiar insecurity and self-doubt that had long defined her began to melt away, at least temporarily, replaced by a newfound focus and intensity. Her shoulders straightened, her chin lifted, and in that moment, she caught a glimpse of herself that she scarcely recognized.

The girl staring back at her in the mirror was not the timid, hunched-over figure she had grown accustomed to seeing. Instead, there was a fire in her eyes, a sense of purpose and passion that she had never experienced before. She was alive, determined, and in that instant, she felt a surge of pride and exhilaration that left her breathless.

But just as quickly as the moment had come, it was shattered by the familiar sound of her brothers' laughter drifting up from the living room below. She felt her heart sink, the weight of their ridicule and judgment once again threatening to consume her.

Slowly, she lowered the monologue, her fingers trembling as she smoothed the crumpled pages. The spark of determination that had momentarily ignited within her began to flicker and fade, replaced by the familiar pangs of self-doubt and insecurity.

Yet, even as the shadows of her past threatened to engulf her, Janet couldn't shake the memory of that fleeting moment in the mirror. The unfamiliar fire in her eyes, the sense of purpose and passion that had so briefly taken hold – it was a glimpse of a self she had never known, a self that yearned to be set free.

As she turned to leave the bathroom, Janet paused, her gaze once more settling on her reflection. Reaching out, she gently traced the outline of her own face, a small, determined smile tugging at the corners of her lips.

"I am more than this," she whispered, the words barely audible even to her own ears. "And one day, I'm going to prove it." With that, she took a deep breath and stepped out into the familiar confines of her home, the memory of that spark of passion burning brighter with each passing moment.

The days that followed were a whirlwind of preparation and self-discovery for Janet. After their initial session, she and Liam had continued to meet regularly, each encounter chipping away at the armor of insecurity.

As they gathered in the empty classroom once more, Liam greeted Janet with a warm smile, his eyes shining with a renewed sense of purpose.

"Okay, I've got something a little different for us to work on today," he said, his voice brimming with enthusiasm. "I think it's time we start focusing on your body language and stage presence."

Janet felt a familiar flutter of nerves in the pit of her stomach, her fingers instinctively reaching up to tuck a stray lock of hair behind her ear. The idea of drawing further attention to herself, of potentially putting her insecurities on full display, was both thrilling and deeply unsettling.

Sensing her discomfort, Liam reached out and gently squeezed her arm, his touch both steadying and reassuring.

"Hey, don't worry," he said, his tone soft and encouraging. "We're going to take this one step at a time. I just want you to focus on being present and owning the space, okay?"

Janet nodded, though the tightness in her chest betrayed the anxiety that threatened to consume her. As Liam stepped back, she felt an overwhelming urge to shrink, to make herself as small and inconspicuous as possible.

Slowly, tentatively, she began to move, her shoulders hunched and her gaze fixed firmly on the floor. But Liam's gentle voice soon interrupted her, guiding her through a series of confident postures and movements.

"Stand up tall, Janet," he said, his own body language shifting to demonstrate the desired effect. "Lift your chin, open up your chest. Imagine that you're taking up space, commanding the attention of the room."

Janet felt a surge of self-consciousness wash over her, the weight of Liam's words causing her to tense up even further. But as she observed his fluid, assured movements, a small part of her couldn't help but be captivated.

Cautiously, she began to mirror his actions, straightening her spine and lifting her chin. At first, the unfamiliar sensations felt awkward and unnatural, as if she were wearing a costume that didn't quite fit. But with each passing moment, something began to shift within her.

As she stood taller, Janet felt a strange new power coursing through her veins – a sense of confidence and self-assurance that she had never experienced before. The familiar urge to shrink away and disappear began to fade, replaced by a growing awareness of her own physical presence.

Liam watched intently, his eyes shining with pride and encouragement. "That's it, Janet," he murmured, his voice barely above a whisper. "You're doing great. Just keep focusing on your breath and owning this space."

Janet's gaze met his, and in that moment, she felt a spark of something she had long thought lost – a glimmer of hope and possibility that had been buried beneath the weight of her own insecurities.

Slowly, tentatively, she began to move with more purpose, her steps growing steadier and her posture more assured. And as she did, she couldn't help but marvel at the subtle yet profound shift she felt within herself.

In this moment, Janet wasn't the timid, hunched-over figure she had grown so accustomed to seeing. Instead, she was a young woman who was learning to stand tall, to embrace the fullness of her own being, and to claim the space that was rightfully hers.

It was a small but significant victory, the result of the power of Liam's friendship and the transformative journey she had embarked upon. And as she met his gaze, a small, determined smile tugging at the corners of her lips, Janet knew that she was one step closer to discovering the true depths of her own strength and potential. As the days ticked by and the audition date drew ever closer, she found herself consumed by a whirlwind of emotions. The excitement and determination that had slowly blossomed within her was now tinged with a growing sense of dread and anxiety.

During their daily rehearsals, Liam could sense the shift in Janet's demeanor, the way her shoulders would tense and her gaze would dart nervously around the room. He knew that the weight of her self-doubt was beginning to take its toll, and he was determined to do whatever it took to help her through it.

One afternoon, as they sat together in the cafeteria, Liam couldn't help but notice the way Janet was pushing the food around on her tray, her brow furrowed with a deep, pensive frown.

Hey, he said softly, reaching out to gently touch her arm. "What's going on? You seem a little off today."

Janet lifted her gaze, her eyes shimmering with a mix of emotions that Liam couldn't quite decipher. For a moment, she was silent, her fingers fidgeting nervously with the edge of her sleeve.

"I'm... I'm just so scared, Liam," she finally whispered, her voice barely audible over the din of the crowded lunchroom. "What if I mess up? What if they all laugh at me again, like they always do?"

Liam's heart ached at the raw vulnerability in her words, the way her voice trembled with a lifetime of hurt and self-doubt. Shifting closer, he reached out and covered her hand with his own, his touch both steadying and reassuring.

"Janet," he said, his tone gentle and understanding. "I know how terrifying this must feel. But I want you to know that I'm here for you, every step of the way."

Janet lifted her gaze, her eyes shimmering with unshed tears. "You... you do?" she asked, the words barely above a whisper.

Liam nodded, his expression open and sincere. "Of course I do," he replied. "And you know, I've been there too – the stage fright, the fear of failure. It's something I've had to work through myself."

Janet's eyes widened with surprise, and Liam could see the flicker of understanding dawning on her face. Slowly, he continued, his words measured and heartfelt.

"I know how easy it is to get caught up in those negative thoughts, to convince yourself that you're not good enough. But Janet, you are so much more than that. You have a strength and a resilience that I truly admire."

As the words left his lips, Liam watched as the walls of Janet's carefully constructed facade began to crumble. In that moment, the weight of her secret shame and self-doubt seemed to lift, and she opened up in a way she never had before.

"My brothers," she began, her voice trembling with emotion. "They've always made fun of me, told me I'm not good enough. And I... I guess I just started to believe them."

Liam listened intently, his heart aching for the young woman sitting before him. Reaching out, he gently squeezed her hand, offering a silent gesture of support and understanding.

Janet continued, the words flowing freely now, as if a dam had been broken. "I'm just so tired of feeling like I have to hide, of always being afraid of what people will think of me. I want to be brave, Liam. I want to be able to stand up and show the world who I really am."

Liam felt a surge of pride and admiration wash over him, and without hesitation, he pulled Janet into a warm, comforting embrace. In that moment, he knew that the walls she had so carefully constructed were beginning to crumble, and that the true essence of who she was – a resilient, determined young woman – was finally starting to emerge.

As they pulled apart, Liam met Janet's gaze, his eyes shining with a newfound understanding and respect.

"You are brave, Janet," he said, his voice steady. "And I'm going to be right here, cheering you on every step of the way. Whatever happens, know that I believe in you, and I'm so proud of you for having the courage to even try."

Janet felt a wave of emotion wash over her, and in that moment, she knew that the weight of her secret shame and self-doubt had lifted, if only slightly. With Liam's constant support and understanding, she felt a newfound sense of strength and determination taking root within her, fueling her resolve to confront her fears and embrace the fullness of her own identity.

As the sun dipped below the horizon, casting long shadows across the quiet suburban streets, Janet lay awake in her bed, her mind consumed by a whirlwind of anxious thoughts. The audition was tomorrow, and the weight of her own self-doubt threatened to suffocate her.

Tossing and turning, she tried in vain to find a comfortable position, but the familiar demons of her past refused to be silenced. Visions of herself on the stage, fumbling over her lines as the audience erupted in laughter, played out in her mind in vivid, terrifying detail.

Janet felt her heart pounding in her chest, the sound echoing in her ears as a cold sweat beaded on her brow. The fear of public humiliation, of once again being the target of her peers' cruel ridicule, was a weight that threatened to crush her.

Squeezing her eyes shut, she tried to push the images away, to focus on the progress she had made, the newfound confidence that had slowly blossomed within her. But the voices of her brothers, the dismissive glances of her classmates, were like a chorus of doubt, drowning out any glimmer of hope.

Suddenly, Janet's eyes snapped open, and she reached for her phone, her fingers trembling as she navigated to Liam's number. In that moment, the temptation to give up, to text him and admit defeat, was almost overwhelming.

But just as she was about to press send, a soft chime interrupted her, and she glanced down to see a new message from Liam, the words shining like a beacon in the darkness.

"Remember, you've already shown so much courage just by deciding to try. Whatever happens tomorrow, I'm proud of you."

Janet felt her breath catch in her throat as she read the message, his words resonating over her in a wave of emotion. For so long, she had been conditioned to doubt her own worth, to shrink away from any opportunity that might expose her to judgment and ridicule.

But in this moment, with Liam's words echoing in her mind, Janet felt a shift within her. The crippling fear that had threatened to consume her began to recede, replaced by a newfound sense of determination and resolve.

Slowly, she read the message again, her fingers tracing the words as if to etch them into her very being. "You've already shown so much courage," Liam had written. And in that instant, Janet realized that he was right – she had already taken the first steps on a journey of self-discovery, and that in itself was an act of bravery.

The memory of her transformation in the theater, the way she had straightened her spine and lifted her chin, filled her with a sense of pride and accomplishment. And as she contemplated the audition that lay ahead, she knew that she was no longer the same timid, insecure girl she had once been.

With a deep, steadying breath, Janet set her phone aside, her gaze fixed on the ceiling above. Tomorrow, she would face her fears head-on, embracing the fullness of her own voice and the depth of her own emotions. And no matter the outcome, she knew that Liam would be there, offering his unconditional support and belief in her.

As the night wore on and the first rays of dawn began to peek through her curtains, Janet felt a renewed sense of purpose and determination take hold. She was ready to take the stage, to shed the constraints of her own self-doubt and embrace the power of her own story.

And with Liam's words echoing in her mind, she knew that she was not alone – that she had the strength and the courage to face whatever challenges lay ahead, one step at a time. The morning of the audition dawned bright and clear, but for Janet, the world seemed to move in a haze of anxiety and anticipation. As she dressed, her fingers trembled with a mix of excitement and dread, and she found herself constantly glancing at the clock, willing the hands to slow their relentless march towards the appointed time.

When the moment finally arrived, Janet stepped out into the crisp autumn air, her gaze immediately drawn to the familiar figure of Liam, who stood waiting for her just outside the theater's entrance. As their eyes met, Liam's face broke into a warm, reassuring smile, and Janet felt a flutter of relief wash over her.

"Liam," she breathed, her voice barely above a whisper. "I'm... I'm so nervous."

Reaching out, Liam gently placed a hand on her shoulder, his touch both steadying and comforting. "I know," he said, his tone soft and understanding. "But you've got this, Janet. I believe in you."

Slowly, Liam's hand dipped into the pocket of his jacket, and when it emerged, he was holding a small, smooth stone, its surface adorned with a single word – "Courage" – painted in bold, vibrant strokes.

"Here," he said, placing the stone in Janet's trembling palm. "I want you to hold onto this. It's a reminder that you've already shown so much bravery just by being here."

Janet felt a lump rise in her throat as she gazed down at the stone, its solid weight a tangible anchor in the swirling storm of her emotions. Closing her fingers around it, she drew strength from its presence, the simple gesture grounding her in the moment.

Together, Janet and Liam made their way towards the theater's entrance, the familiar sounds of voices and the occasional burst of laughter spilling out into the crisp autumn air. As they stepped through the doors, Janet felt a surge of trepidation, her eyes instinctively scanning the bustling waiting area.

To her surprise, she found that the other auditionees were a diverse mix of confidence and nervousness, their expressions mirroring the very emotions that threatened to consume her. Some paced the floor, their movements quick and agitated, while others sat quietly, their gazes fixed on the pages of their scripts.

Janet felt a sense of kinship with these strangers, a shared understanding of the weight of their own self-doubt and the fear of failure. In that moment, she realized that she was not alone in her struggle, that the journey she had embarked upon was one that resonated with so many others.

Clutching the smooth stone in her palm, Janet took a deep, steadying breath, her gaze once more finding Liam's. In his eyes, she saw a reflection of her own determination, a silent promise that no matter what happened, he would be there to support her every step of the way.

With a sense of purpose, Janet stepped further into the theater, her heart pounding in her chest as she prepared to face the challenges that lay ahead. But in the face of her fears, she felt hope and strength ignite within her. The minutes ticked by with agonizing slowness as Janet sat in the bustling waiting area, her fingers clutching the smooth stone in her palm like a lifeline. All around her, the other auditionees shifted nervously, their whispered conversations and the occasional burst of laughter creating a symphony of anticipation and uncertainty.

Suddenly, a hush fell over the room as a name was called, and Janet felt her heart leap into her throat. Glancing up, she watched as a young woman rose on trembling legs and made her way towards the stage, her expression a mix of determination and terror.

Janet couldn't help but empathize with the girl's plight, the weight of her own self-doubt and fears mirrored in the tense set of her shoulders and the anxious glint in her eyes. But as the girl stepped into the spotlight, her voice rang out with a surprising confidence and clarity, captivating the audience with the raw emotion of her performance.

Watching in awe, Janet felt a surge of admiration and inspiration wash over her. If this girl, with all her evident nerves, could find the courage to step into the breach, then perhaps – just perhaps – she could do the same.

As the girl's audition came to a close, the theater erupted in thunderous applause, and Janet couldn't help but join in, her own heart swelling with a newfound sense of determination. She was next, and the thought both thrilled and terrified her.

Suddenly, her name was called, and Janet felt her legs tremble as she rose from her seat. Glancing towards the stage, she caught Liam's eye, and in that moment, she saw a reflection of her own fears and uncertainties – but also a deep, strong belief in her abilities.

Liam gave her a reassuring thumbs up, his lips forming the silent words, "You've got this."

Taking a deep, steadying breath, Janet stepped forward, her fingers tightening around the smooth stone as she made her way towards the stage. With each step, the weight of her own self-doubt seemed to grow heavier, the familiar voices of her brothers and her peers echoing in her mind.

But then, as she crossed the threshold and stepped into the blinding glare of the spotlight, something shifted within her. The noise of doubts and fears that threatened to consume her before began to fade, replaced by a strange, serene calm.

For a moment, Janet felt disoriented, her eyes struggling to adjust to the brightness of the stage. But as her gaze swept over the sea of expectant faces, she was drawn to the reassuring presence of Liam, who has helped her through the storm of her own emotions.

Slowly, she opened her mouth, and to her own amazement, her voice rang out clear and strong, filling the theater with the words she had practiced so diligently. Gone was the timid, hesitant girl who had once shrunk away from the spotlight – in her place stood a young woman who had found the courage to embrace the full-ness of her own voice and the depth of her own emotions.

As she continued to speak, Janet felt a surge of exhilaration and pride wash over her. This was her moment, her chance to shed the constraints of her own self-doubt and truly be seen and heard. And in that instant, she knew that she had discovered a part of herself she never knew existed – a part that was unafraid, unapologetic, and entirely her own.

The thunderous applause that erupted as she finished her audition was a testament to the power of her performance, but for Janet, the true victory lay in the transformation she had undergone. In this moment, she was no longer defined by the limitations of her past, but by the boundless potential of her future.

With a newfound sense of purpose and determination, Janet stepped off the stage, her gaze immediately seeking out Liam. And as their eyes met, she saw a reflection of her own triumph – a spark of pride and admiration that filled her with a sense of validation and belonging she had never experienced before.

In that instant, Janet knew that her life had been forever changed, and that the journey she had embarked upon was only just beginning.

STEPPING INTO THE SPOTLIGHT

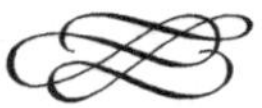

Janet stood backstage at the community theater, her heart pounding in her chest. The familiar weight of Liam's good luck charm felt like an anchor in her trembling hand, a tangible reminder of the support and encouragement that had carried her this far.

As the sounds of the audience settling into their seats drifted through the curtain, Janet felt a surge of both excitement and terror. This was it – the moment she had been preparing for, the chance to shed the constraints of her own self-doubt and embrace the fullness of her voice.

Closing her eyes, Janet took a deep, steadying breath, willing her racing thoughts to slow. In the quiet stillness of the backstage area, she could hear the faint murmur of the crowd, a mixture of symphony of anticipation and expectation that threatened to overwhelm her.

Slowly, she opened her eyes, her gaze immediately drawn to the mirror that stood nearby. The reflection that stared back at her was both familiar and foreign – the timid, hunched-over figure she had grown so accustomed to seeing had been replaced by a young woman whose eyes burned with a newfound determination.

Janet traced the outline of her own face, marveling at the subtle shift in her expression. Gone was the constant worry and self-doubt that had once etched itself into her brow; in its place, a steely resolve that she scarcely recognized.

At that moment, the stage manager's voice rang out, announcing the final countdown to curtain. Janet felt her heart leap into her throat, the weight of the impending performance sending a fresh wave of anxiety coursing through her veins.

But as she clutched Liam's charm, the memory of his unwavering belief in her steadied her nerves. She could still hear his words echoing in her mind, a gentle reminder of the strength and resilience she had discovered within herself.

"You've got this, Janet," he had told her, his voice brimming with pride and encouragement. "Just be yourself up there, and let your voice be heard."

Taking one last deep breath, Janet closed her eyes and began to silently recite her lines, her lips moving with a quiet determination. In the darkness behind her lids, she could see the characters and scenes she had so meticulously rehearsed, each word and gesture etched into her memory.

As the final seconds ticked away, she felt a strange sense of calm wash over her. The frantic beating of her heart began to slow, and the familiar knot of anxiety in the pit of her stomach began to unravel.

In this moment, she was no longer the timid, insecure girl who had once shrunk away from the spotlight. She was a young woman who had found the courage to step into the breach, to confront her fears and embrace the fullness of her own identity.

With a renewed sense of purpose, Janet opened her eyes, her gaze sweeping across the familiar backstage area. The stage manager stood nearby, a reassuring smile on his face as he gave her a subtle nod.

"You've got this, Janet," he murmured, his words echoing Liam's sentiment. "Break a leg out there."

Janet felt the corners of her lips tug upwards in a small, determined smile. Clutching Liam's charm tightly, she squared her shoulders and stepped forward, ready to face the unknown that lay beyond the curtain. The curtain rose, and Janet stepped out onto the stage, momentarily blinded by the bright lights that illuminated the vast theater. For a split second, panic threatened to overwhelm her, and she felt her heart pounding in her chest.

But then, as her eyes adjusted to the glare, she was captivated by the sea of faces that stretched out before her. Hundreds of pairs of eyes were fixed upon her, the weight of their collective gaze both thrilling and terrifying.

Gripping Liam's good luck charm tighter in her palm, Janet took a deep, steadying breath. She could feel the smooth surface of the stone against her skin, a tangible reminder of the support and encouragement that had carried her to this moment.

Steeling her nerves, Janet opened her mouth and began to speak, her voice ringing out clear and strong, filling the theater. To her own amazement, the words flowed effortlessly, each line delivered with a newfound confidence and conviction that she scarcely recognized.

As she continued, Janet felt herself settling into the character, her fears and insecurities slowly melting away. The familiar lines she had rehearsed countless times now took on a life of their own, infused with a depth of emotion that she had never before experienced.

Gone was the timid, hesitant girl who had once shrunk away from the spotlight. In her place stood a young woman who had found the courage to step into the breach, to embrace the fullness of her own voice and the power of her own story.

With each passing moment, Janet felt a sense of exhilaration and liberation wash over her. The bright lights that had once blinded her now seemed to illuminate the very essence of who she was, stripping away the layers of self-doubt and insecurity that had long defined her.

In this moment, she was no longer bound by the limitations of her past or the expectations of those around her. She was simply Janet, a young woman who had discovered the transformative power of finding her voice and owning her truth.

As she moved across the stage, her movements growing more assured with each passing line, Janet felt a profound sense of connection with the character she was portraying. The raw emotions that had once threatened to consume her now fueled her performance, lending a depth and authenticity that captivated the audience.

In the sea of faces that stretched out before her, Janet caught glimpses of rapt attention, of awe and admiration that filled her with a sense of validation and pride. Gone were the taunts and dismissive glances of her past; in their place, a newfound respect and appreciation that left her breathless.

For the first time in her life, Janet felt truly seen and heard, her voice resonating with a power and conviction that she had scarcely imagined possible. And as she lost herself in the performance, she knew that this was only the beginning – a testament to the transformative journey that lay ahead. As the play progressed, Janet was immersed in a pivotal scene, one that called upon her to deliver a powerful, emotional monologue. The weight of the words, the depth of the character's pain and insecurity, resonated with her in a way she had never anticipated.

With a steadying breath, Janet stepped forward, her gaze sweeping across the captivated audience. In that moment, the bright lights that had once seemed so blinding now felt like a warm embrace, illuminating the very essence of her performance.

As she began to speak, Janet felt a shift within her, a connection to the character's raw emotions that seemed to transcend the boundaries of the stage. The words flowed from her lips with a raw, unfiltered honesty, each syllable imbued with the weight of her own experiences.

The audience fell silent, their eyes fixed upon her, hanging on her every word. Janet could feel the tension in the air, the palpable sense of anticipation that seemed to hold them all in thrall.

And as she continued, something profound began to unfold within her. The barriers she had so carefully constructed, the walls of insecurity and self-doubt that had long defined her, began to crumble. In their place, a wellspring of emotion surged forth, a cathartic release that left her feeling both vulnerable and empowered.

In this moment, Janet was no longer simply reciting lines or embodying a character. She was giving voice to the pain and anguish she had carried for so long, the scars left by the taunts and ridicule that had once threatened to consume her.

The audience remained transfixed, their expressions had a mix of awe, empathy, and understanding. And for the first time in her life, Janet felt truly seen, her story resonating with a depth and authenticity that left her breathless.

As the final words of the monologue left her lips, a hush fell over the theater, the silence so profound that it seemed to echo in the very marrow of her bones. And then, like the first drops of a gathering storm, the sound of applause began to swell, building in a crescendo that washed over her in a wave of validation and triumph.

Janet felt a profound sense of catharsis, a release of the pain and insecurity that had long held her captive. She had found her voice, her truth, and in doing so, had unlocked a part of herself that she had scarcely dared to imagine.

The audience's thunderous applause was a testament to the power of her performance, but for Janet, the true victory lay in the transformation she had undergone – a metamorphosis that had stripped away the constraints of her past and allowed her to embrace the fullness of her own identity. As the play progressed, Janet felt a newfound sense of confidence blossoming within her. With each passing scene, the initial trepidation and self-doubt began to melt away, replaced by a growing assurance and creativity.

No longer content to simply recite her lines, Janet was improvising small gestures and subtle inflections, imbuing her character with a depth and authenticity that she had scarcely dared to explore during the rehearsals.

The energy between her and her fellow cast members was electric, a palpable synergy that seemed to feed off the audience's rapt attention. Together, they moved as one, each performer feeding off the others' energy and passion, creating a storytelling masterpiece that had everyone hooked.

Janet felt herself swept up in the sheer joy of collaborative performance, the boundaries between herself and the character she portrayed blurring until she could scarcely tell where one ended and the other began. In this moment, she was no longer simply an actress on a stage; she was a vessel for a story that demanded to be told, a conduit for the raw emotions that pulsed through the very heart of the production.

As she moved with a newfound fluidity, her gestures and expressions becoming more natural and instinctive, Janet marveled at the transformation she was undergoing. The timid, insecure girl, had been replaced by a young woman who embraced the stage, who reveled in the opportunity to share her voice and her truth with the world.

The audience, too, seemed to sense the shift, their reactions growing more animated and engaged with each passing moment. Laughter, gasps, and murmurs of approval punctuated the performance, a harmony of emotional responses that fueled Janet's performance and spurred her on to greater heights.

She was no longer simply acting; she was living, breathing, and embodying the very essence of the character she portrayed. The lines between reality and fiction had blurred, and Janet found herself lost in the sheer exhilaration of the experience, her fears and insecurities fading into the background as she surrendered herself to the power of the story.

As the scene drew to a close, the audience erupted again in thunderous applause, their enthusiasm a confirmation of the transformative journey they had witnessed. And in the midst of the ovation, Janet caught the eye of her fellow cast members, their expressions mirroring the sense of pride and accomplishment that swelled within her.

In that instant, she knew that she had found her true calling, a passion that had the power to transcend the limitations of her past and unlock the fullest expression of her own identity. And with each passing moment, the joy of collaborative storytelling continued to fuel her, propelling her ever forward on a journey of self-discovery and transformation. As the first act drew to a close, Janet retreated to a quiet corner backstage, the rush of adrenaline and emotion leaving her feeling both exhilarated and overwhelmed.

The thunderous applause that had echoed through the theater still reverberated in her ears, evidence to the power of her performance. But beneath the surface, Janet felt a swirling maelstrom of conflicting emotions – pride, disbelief, and a lingering sense of uncertainty that refused to be silenced.

Leaning against the cool, concrete wall, Janet took a deep, steadying breath, her fingers tracing the smooth surface of Liam's good luck charm. The familiar weight of the stone was a grounding presence, a tangible reminder of the support and encouragement that had carried her to this moment.

Suddenly, a familiar voice broke the silence, and Janet glanced up to see Liam approaching, his face beaming with a sense of pride and admiration.

"Janet, that was amazing!" he exclaimed. "You were incredible out there."

Janet felt a flush of warmth spread across her cheeks, the weight of Liam's praise both thrilling and humbling. For so long, she had conditioned herself to deflect any form of positive attention, to dismiss the compliments of others as mere platitudes. But at that moment, seeing the gleam in Liam's eyes, she was unable to deny the truth of his words.

"You really think so?" she asked, her voice barely above a whisper. "I just... I can't believe I actually did it."

Liam nodded emphatically, his hand reaching out to gently squeeze her arm. "Believe it, Janet," he said, his tone warm and reassuring. "You were absolutely captivating out there. I'm so proud of you."

Janet felt a surge of emotion well up within her, the weight of Liam's words cutting through the lingering doubts and insecurities. In this moment, she allowed herself to bask in the glow of his praise, to let go of the need to deflect or diminish her own accomplishments.

"Thank you, Liam," she whispered, her voice thick with emotion. "I couldn't have done it without you."

The two of them shared a moment of quiet celebration, their eyes locked in a silent exchange of triumph and understanding. In that instant, Janet felt a profound sense of connection, a kinship that transcended the boundaries of their friendship and spoke to the very core of their shared journey.

All too soon, the stage manager's voice rang out, signaling the impending start of the second act. Reluctantly, Janet and Liam parted ways, each carrying the weight of the moment with them as they prepared to take the stage once more.

But as Janet stepped back into the bright lights, she felt a renewed sense of purpose and determination coursing through her veins. The doubts and fears that had once threatened to consume her had been replaced by a burning desire to embrace the fullness of her own voice and the power of her own story.

And with Liam's firm support and belief echoing in her mind, she knew that she was ready to face whatever challenges lay ahead, one step at a time. As the play reached its climactic finale, Janet poured every ounce of herself into her performance, her focus laser-sharp and her emotions raw and unfiltered.

Gone were the lingering doubts and insecurities. In their place, a burning determination and a profound sense of purpose that fueled her every word and gesture.

No longer was she simply reciting lines or embodying a character; in this moment, Janet was fully immersed in the world of the story, her own experiences and emotions intertwining with those of the character she portrayed.

The audience, once a sea of expectant faces, faded into the background as Janet lost herself in the power of the performance. The weight of their collective gaze no longer filled her with trepidation, but rather, a sense of validation and purpose that drove her forward.

When the time came for her pivotal speech, Janet opened her mouth, and the words flowed forth with a raw, unfiltered honesty that left the audience spellbound. Gone were the tentative, hesitant tones that had once defined her; in their place, a voice that rang out with a conviction and passion that seemed to reverberate in the very walls of the theater.

As the final syllables left her lips, the audience fell into a stunned silence, the weight of her performance hanging in the air like a palpable presence. And then, like the first drops of a gathering storm, the sound of thunderous applause erupted once again, washing over Janet in a wave of validation and triumph.

As the thunderous applause continued to echo in the distance through her performance, Janet felt a surge of pride and accomplishment wash over her. She had faced her fears, confronted the demons of her past, and emerged triumphant – a testament to the resilience and strength that had been there all along, waiting to be unleashed. As the final curtain fell, the cast gathered together for their curtain call, the roar of the audience's applause echoing through the theater. Janet felt a surge of anticipation and trepidation as her name was called, signaling her turn to step forward and take her bow.

With a deep, steadying breath, she moved to the front of the stage, her gaze sweeping across the sea of faces that stretched out before her. And in that moment, she felt a profound shift within her – the timid, insecure girl she had once been was nowhere to be found, replaced by a young woman whose eyes shone with a newfound confidence and pride.

As Janet stepped forward, the audience erupted in a thunderous standing ovation, the sound of their applause washing over her in a wave of validation and triumph. For so long, she had craved this moment, this validation of her worth and her abilities. But now, as she stood there, basking in the adoration of the crowd, she realized that the true victory lay not in their approval, but in the transformation she had undergone.

Janet felt a surge of pride and accomplishment unlike anything she had ever experienced, a profound sense of self-worth that seemed to radiate from the very core of her being. Gone were the lingering doubts and insecurities that had once defined her; in their place, a deep firm belief in her own capabilities and the power of her own voice.

Tears of joy and relief streamed down her face as the curtain fell, the roar of the crowd a confirmation of the transformative journey she had undertaken. In this moment, Janet was no longer the timid, insecure girl who had once shrunk away from the spotlight.

As she scanned the audience, her gaze landed upon a familiar sight – her family, seated in the front row! Her parents' faces were alight with pride, their eyes shining with a depth of emotion that left Janet feeling both humbled and emboldened. And even her brothers, whose taunts and ridicule had once been the bane of her existence, were looking on with an expression of begrudging respect and admiration.

In that moment, Janet felt a weight lift from her shoulders, a lifetime of pain and resentment finally beginning to dissipate. The journey she had undertaken had not been an easy one, but in facing her fears and embracing the fullness of her own identity, she had discovered a strength and resilience that she had scarcely dared to imagine.

As the applause continued to thunder around her, Janet allowed herself to bask in the glow of her triumph, her heart swelling with a profound sense of gratitude and accomplishment. This was her moment, her story, and she had claimed it with a courage and conviction that had transformed not only her own life, but the lives of those around her.

In the days and weeks that followed, Janet would carry the memory of this night with her, a beacon of hope and inspiration that would guide her through the challenges that still lay ahead. But in this moment, as she stood before the adoring crowd, she knew that she had found her voice, and that nothing would ever be the same again. As the curtain fell and the thunderous applause began to subside.

Backstage, the cast gathered, their expressions a mixture of pride and exhilaration. Janet felt herself enveloped in a chorus of congratulations and well-wishes, the warmth of their embrace a tangible reflection of the bond they had forged through the shared experience of collaborative storytelling.

In the theater lobby, Janet was swept up in a whirlwind of well-wishers. Cast members, audience members, and even the director himself approached her, their faces alight with praise and admiration.

"That was an incredible performance!" one audience member exclaimed, her eyes shining with genuine enthusiasm. "You had us all on the edge of our seats."

Janet felt a flush of warmth spread across her cheeks, the weight of the positive attention both thrilling and overwhelming. For so long, she had craved this validation, this recognition of her worth and her abilities. But now, as the accolades poured in, she handled it with a newfound grace and confidence that surprised even her.

Gone was the timid, self-conscious girl who had once shrunk away from the spotlight. In her place stood a young woman who carried herself with a quiet assurance, her gaze steady and her smile warm and genuine.

As she moved through the crowd, accepting the well-wishes and congratulations with a poise that belied her years, Janet couldn't help but marvel at the transformation she had undergone. The journey that had brought her to this moment had been arduous, filled with challenges and self-doubt that had threatened to consume her. But in the end, she had emerged victorious, her voice and her identity reclaimed with a strength and conviction that left her breathless.

Suddenly, her gaze landed upon a familiar face across the room, and Janet felt a surge of emotion wash over her. There, amid the throng of well-wishers, stood Liam, his expression full of pride and triumph.

Their eyes met, and in that moment, a silent understanding passed between them – a shared acknowledgment of the transformative journey they had undertaken, and the profound impact it had left upon both of their lives.

Janet felt a smile tug at the corners of her lips, and without a word, she made her way through the crowd, her steps sure and steady. As she reached Liam, she felt a sense of profound gratitude and affection swell within her for all the support and encouragement he had provided throughout her journey.

"Thank you," she whispered, her voice thick with emotion. "For everything."

Liam's expression softened, and he reached out, gently squeezing her arm in a gesture of reassurance and camaraderie. "You did this, Janet," he replied, his tone warm and sincere. "I'm just honored to have been a part of it."

The two of them shared a smile of triumph, both knowing that this night marked a significant turning point in Janet's life. The barriers that had once confined her had crumbled, and in their place, a newfound sense of confidence and self-acceptance had taken root – a confirmation to the power of finding one's voice and embracing the fullness of one's own identity.

As Janet moved on to greet the next well-wisher, she felt a profound sense of gratitude and purpose coursing through her veins. The journey had been long and arduous, but in the end, she had emerged victorious, her voice and her story reclaimed with a strength and conviction that would continue to guide her for years to come.

Janet stepped through the front door, her heart still racing from the exhilaration of her performance. The theater had been a sanctuary, a place where she had discovered the power of her own voice and the courage to embrace her true self. But as she entered the familiar confines of her home, the weight of her past threatened to come crashing down upon her.

The house was eerily silent, devoid of the usual taunts and jeers that had long defined her existence. Janet paused, her gaze sweeping across the empty living room, a sense of unease settling in the pit of her stomach. Where were her brothers, the relentless tormentors who had made her life a living hell?

Cautiously, she made her way up the stairs, her footsteps muffled by the plush carpet. As she reached the landing, she caught a glimpse of her reflection in the hallway mirror, and for the first time in years, she allowed herself a genuine smile. The confident, assured young woman staring back at her was a far cry from the timid, insecure girl she had once been.

But the moment of triumph was short-lived. Suddenly, the silence was shattered by a cruel comment from one of her brothers, his voice dripping with disdain as he passed by her open door.

"Well, look who's finally decided to grace us with her presence. Didn't think you'd have the nerve to show your face around here after your little performance."

Janet felt the blood drain from her face, the familiar sting of her brother's words cutting through the fragile veil of her newfound confidence. Her hands trembled as she gripped the doorframe, the weight of her past threatening to consume her once more.

In that moment, the exhilaration of her theater triumph felt like a distant memory, overshadowed by the crushing reality of the life she had been forced to endure. The taunts, the ridicule, the relentless assault on her self-worth – it all came rushing back, a torrent of emotions that threatened to overwhelm her.

Janet closed her eyes, willing herself to find the strength that had carried her through the performance. But the familiar voices of her brothers, their cruel laughter echoing in the hallway, made it impossible to hold onto the sense of empowerment she had felt on stage.

Slowly, she sank down onto the edge of her bed, her shoulders hunched in defeat. The quiet triumph she had allowed herself just moments ago had been shattered, replaced by the familiar ache of self-doubt and insecurity.

As she sat there, staring blankly at the wall, Janet felt the weight of her past pressing down upon her, a constant reminder of the battles she had yet to face. The journey she had undertaken, the transformation she had undergone – it all seemed to crumble in the face of her brothers' relentless taunts.

But deep within her, a glimmer of resolve began to flicker. The memory of the thunderous applause, the validation she had felt on the stage, refused to be extinguished. And as she drew a shaky breath, Janet knew that she could not – would not – allow her brothers to rob her of the hard-won confidence she had discovered.

With a renewed sense of determination, she rose from the bed, her gaze hardening as she made her way to the door. The time had come to confront her past, to stand up to the demons that had haunted her for so long. And this time, she would not back down.

Janet awoke the next morning, the lingering euphoria of her theater performance still coursing through her veins. But as she reached down to retrieve her backpack, her hand brushed against a stack of crumpled notes that had been slipped under her door.

Dread pooled in the pit of her stomach as she unfolded the pages, her eyes scanning the cruel words scrawled across the paper. Her brothers had struck again, their taunts and insults a vicious retaliation against her moment in the spotlight.

Janet's hands trembled as she read the mocking comments about her appearance, the familiar sting of their words cutting deep. The confidence she had felt the night before began to crumble, replaced by a crushing sense of self-doubt and insecurity.

She had been so sure of herself, so empowered by the experience of standing on that stage and sharing her voice with the world. But now, in the harsh light of day, the weight of her siblings' cruelty threatened to overshadow all that she had accomplished.

Tears welled in Janet's eyes as she sat on the edge of her bed, the notes clutched tightly in her hands. A part of her wanted to march downstairs and confront her brothers, to finally stand up to the relentless bullying that had defined her life. But the fear of making things worse, of opening herself up to even more ridicule, held her back.

Maybe she should confide in her parents, she thought, her gaze drifting towards the closed bedroom door. But the memory of all the times she had tried to speak up, only to be dismissed or ignored, made her stomach twist with dread.

As she prepared for school, Janet struggled to hold onto the confidence she had felt the night before. Her brothers' jeers echoed in her mind, a constant reminder of the fragility of her newfound self-assurance. With a deep, steadying breath, she squared her shoulders and headed out the door, determined to face the day with the same resilience that had carried her through the performance.

But the weight of the crumpled notes in her backpack felt like a heavy burden, a constant reminder of the battles she had yet to fight. As she walked, Janet couldn't help but wonder if the triumph she had tasted on the stage was nothing more than a fleeting moment, soon to be overshadowed by the relentless onslaught of her siblings' cruelty. As Janet stepped onto the school grounds, the familiar weight of her brothers' taunts felt like a heavy cloak draped over her shoulders. She scanned the bustling hallways, her eyes searching for a familiar face – someone who could offer a respite from the relentless onslaught of cruelty she faced at home.

And then, she spotted Liam, his kind eyes and gentle demeanor a beacon of hope in the chaos. Hurrying towards him, Janet felt a surge of relief, her voice trembling as she reached into her backpack and pulled out the crumpled notes.

"Liam, I... I need your help," she whispered, her gaze downcast as she handed him the pages. "My brothers, they're... they're worse than ever."

Liam's expression darkened as he read the cruel words, his usual calm demeanor slipping as the full extent of Janet's home life became clear. His hands tightened around the notes, a flash of anger flaring in his eyes.

"Janet, this is unacceptable," he said, his voice low and urgent. "You can't keep letting them treat you this way. Have you talked to your parents? Or maybe a teacher or counselor?"

But at the mention of involving others, recoiled, the fear of making the situation even worse overwhelmed her. "No, I can't," she pleaded, her eyes wide with panic. "They'll just make it worse, I know they will."

Liam's brow furrowed with concern, his gaze searching Janet's face as he tried to understand the depth of her reluctance. After a moment, he reached out and gently squeezed her arm, his touch a silent offer of support.

"Okay, we'll figure this out," he said, his voice soft and reassuring. "But you can't keep letting them walk all over you, Janet. You deserve so much better than this."

As the warning bell rang, signaling the start of the school day, Liam and Janet parted ways, their eyes locking in a silent exchange. Liam's gaze was filled with a mixture of worry and determination, his mind already racing with ways to help his friend.

Janet felt a pang of guilt, knowing that she was burdening Liam with the weight of her struggles. But in that moment, the warmth of his concern was a lifeline, a glimmer of hope in the darkness that threatened to consume her.

With a deep breath, Janet squared her shoulders and headed to class, the crumpled notes still clutched tightly in her hand. She knew that the battle ahead would be arduous, but with Liam by her side, she felt a newfound resolve taking root – a determination to confront her past and reclaim the power that had been stolen from her.

The cafeteria was abuzz with the familiar din of lunchtime chatter, but as Janet made her way to the table where her theater group sat, a sense of calm washed over her. Here, in the company of her friends, she felt a glimmer of the confidence and self-assurance that had carried her through the performance the night before.

Settling into her seat, she basked in the praise and camaraderie of her theater companions, their enthusiastic congratulations a balm to the lingering wounds inflicted by her brothers' cruelty. For a fleeting moment, she allowed herself to bask in the warmth of their acceptance, the weight of her past struggles momentarily lifted from her shoulders.

But the fragile bubble of peace was shattered by the sudden eruption of mocking laughter from across the cafeteria. Janet's head snapped up, her heart sinking as she recognized the all-too-familiar faces of her brothers and their friends, their eyes gleaming with a malicious intent.

Instinctively, Janet shrank in her seat, the confidence she had felt on stage evaporating in an instant. The jeers and taunts that had once defined her everyday life now seemed to echo through the cavernous space, drowning out the chatter of her theater companions.

But as Janet's gaze darted around the table, she was met with a sight that left her both touched and emboldened. Her friends, sensing her distress, had rallied around her, creating a protective circle that shielded her from the prying eyes of her tormentors.

The gesture, simple yet profoundly meaningful, struck a chord deep within Janet's heart. In that moment, she caught a glimpse of what true friendship and support could feel like — a sanctuary where she could be her authentic self, free from the constant fear of judgment and ridicule.

As the mocking laughter from her brothers' table continued to reverberate through the cafeteria, Janet felt a surge of gratitude and affection for the people who had chosen to stand by her side. These were not mere acquaintances or casual classmates; they were kindred spirits, bound by a shared experience and a deep understanding of the challenges she faced.

In the face of her brothers' cruelty, Janet's theater friends had chosen to offer her the very thing she had craved for so long - a sense of belonging, to be accepted, and their support. And as she sat there, surrounded by their warmth and solidarity, she felt a glimmer of hope begin to take root, an undeniable proof of the power of community and the transformative potential of finding one's tribe. As the bell rang, Janet made her way to her English class, her mind still reeling from the emotional rollercoaster of the day. The warmth and support she had felt from her theater friends had been a welcome respite, but the lingering sting of her brothers' cruelty continued to weigh heavily on her heart.

Settling into her seat, Janet's gaze drifted to the front of the room, where her English teacher stood, a thoughtful expression on her face. Clearing her throat, the teacher addressed the class, her voice carrying a note of gravity that immediately piqued Janet's interest.

"Today, we're going to be embarking on a new project," the teacher began, her eyes sweeping across the attentive students. "It's a personal narrative assignment, one that I believe has the power to transform not only your writing, but your very understanding of yourselves."

Janet felt a spark of inspiration ignite within her, her mind suddenly buzzing with possibilities. Personal narratives – the very idea seemed to resonate with the experiences she had been grappling with, both on and off the stage.

Janet was captivated as the teacher delved deeper into the assignment, emphasizing the importance of finding one's voice and sharing one's story. She had always viewed her struggles with her brothers as a source of pain and anguish, but now, a new perspective began to take shape.

What if, instead of seeing her experiences as a burden, she could reframe them as a testament to her own resilience and strength? The confidence she had discovered through her theater performance had unlocked a new sense of self-awareness, and she found herself contemplating the power of sharing her story with the world.

Reaching into her bag, she pulled out a notebook and began to jot down ideas, her pen moving across the page with a newfound sense of purpose. But as she sat there, her pen poised over the blank page, Janet felt a renewed sense of determination take root. The voice she had discovered on the stage had given her the courage to consider speaking up about her experiences off stage as well, and she was determined to see this journey through, no matter the obstacles that lay in her path.

As the final bell of the day rang, Janet made her way to the familiar doors of the community theater, her steps quickening with each passing moment. This place, with its vibrant energy and supportive community, had become a sanctuary – a refuge from the relentless torment she faced at school and home.

But as Janet pushed open the heavy doors and stepped inside, she was immediately struck by the sound of raised voices echoing through the lobby. Pausing, she followed the source of the commotion, her curiosity piqued.

There, in the center of the room, stood Liam, his usually calm demeanor replaced by a passionate intensity that Janet had never seen before. He was engaged in a heated discussion with the theater director, his hands gesturing emphatically as he argued his point.

Intrigued, Janet drew closer, straining to hear the words that were being exchanged. And as she listened, her heart swelled with a mixture of gratitude and embarrassment – Liam was advocating for a play that addressed the issue of bullying and its devastating impact on young people.

It was clear that he had been inspired by Janet's own struggles, and the realization that someone cared so deeply about her plight left her feeling both touched and exposed.

Hesitantly, Janet stepped forward, her presence interrupting the heated exchange. Both Liam and the director turned to face her, their expressions shifting from intensity to concern.

"Janet," Liam breathed, his eyes widening with a mixture of surprise and relief. "I... I was just talking to the director about a play idea. One that could make a real difference for people like you."

The director's gaze softened as he regarded Janet, a thoughtful expression settling upon his features. "Is this something you'd be interested in exploring, Janet?" he asked, his voice gentle and inviting.

In that moment, Janet felt a surge of emotions swirling within her. Part of her wanted to shrink away, to avoid the vulnerability that came with sharing her story. But another part, a part that had been nurtured and strengthened by her experiences on stage, urged her to step forward and embrace this opportunity.

Taking a deep breath, Janet lifted her chin, her eyes meeting the director's with a newfound sense of resolve. "Yes," she said, her voice steady and sure. "I think it's time for me to share my story."

The director nodded, a small smile tugging at the corners of his lips. "Then let's talk," he said, gesturing towards a nearby table. "I'm listening."

As Janet sat down, Liam's hand brushed against her arm, a silent gesture of support and encouragement. And in that moment, she knew that she was no longer alone in her fight – that the community she had found within these walls would be there to lift her up, to give her the strength to confront her past and reclaim her voice.

As the sun dipped below the horizon, casting the room in a soft, golden glow, Janet sat at her desk, a blank page staring back at her. The events of the day had left her mind whirling, a kaleidoscope of emotions that demanded to be given voice.

Picking up her pen, Janet poised it over the paper, hesitating for a moment as a wave of trepidation washed over her. To put her experiences, her deepest fears and struggles, down on paper – it was a daunting prospect, one that threatened to unravel the fragile threads of her newfound confidence.

But as the memory of Liam's support and the director's empathetic invitation echoed in her mind, she felt a surge of resolve take root. This was her story, her truth, and it deserved to be heard.

In that moment, Janet realized that the journey she had undertaken, the battles she had fought, were not just a source of personal anguish, but a potential source of inspiration and empowerment. By sharing her story, she could not only heal the wounds of her past, but perhaps even inspire others who had faced similar challenges.

The weight of this revelation settled upon her shoulders, both daunting and exhilarating. Janet knew that the road ahead would not be an easy one, that confronting her past and finding the courage to speak her truth would require a level of vulnerability she had long denied herself.

With a steadying breath, she began to write, the words flowing from her pen with a raw, unfiltered honesty that surprised even her. The pain of her brothers' relentless bullying, the crushing weight of their cruel taunts and dismissive laughter – it all poured out onto the page, a torrent of emotion that had been bottled up for far too long.

Tears streamed down Janet's face as she wrote, her hand trembling with the force of her own vulnerability. The act of putting her experiences into words was both cathartic and agonizing, a release of the shame and silence that had long defined her existence.

As the pages filled, Janet felt a shift within her, a newfound clarity that cut through the haze of her past struggles. She saw her brothers' bullying not just as a source of pain, but as a testament to her own resilience – a challenge that she had faced, and ultimately, overcome.

And in that moment, Janet knew that to truly reclaim her voice, to shatter the cycle of silence and shame that had held her captive, she would need to confront her brothers head-on. The fear and trepidation that had once paralyzed her began to melt away, replaced by a steely determination that burned bright within her heart.

With each word she committed to the page, Janet felt a weight lifting from her shoulders. The act of giving voice to her experiences, of acknowledging the pain and the triumph, was both liberating and empowering. She was no longer the timid, insecure girl who had once shrunk away from the spotlight; she was a young woman who had found the courage to stand up and claim her rightful place in the world.

As the last of the daylight faded, Janet set down her pen, her gaze sweeping across the pages that were now filled with her story. In the quiet solitude of her room, she allowed herself a moment of reflection, a silent acknowledgment of the journey she had undertaken and the battles that still lay ahead.

But this time, she was no longer alone. With the strength she had discovered within herself, Janet knew that she was ready to confront her past and reclaim her voice, once and for all.

The house was cloaked in the stillness of night, the only sound the muffled ticking of the old grandfather clock in the hallway. Janet lay awake in her bed, her mind racing with the events of the day and the weight of the words she had committed to the page.

Unable to find solace in sleep, she quietly slipped out of her room, her footsteps barely audible as she made her way downstairs. A glass of water, she thought, that might be just the thing to calm her restless mind.

But as Janet entered the dimly lit kitchen, she was met with an unexpected sight – her youngest brother, seated at the table, his head bowed. The familiar bravado and arrogance that had once defined him were nowhere to be seen, replaced by a palpable vulnerability that caught Janet off guard.

For a moment, she stood frozen, unsure of how to proceed. This was the very brother who had tormented her relentlessly, whose cruel words and taunts had cut her to the core. And yet, in this quiet, unguarded moment, he seemed almost... human.

Cautiously, Janet approached the table, her footsteps drawing her brother's attention. He lifted his head, his eyes meeting hers, and in that instant, Janet was struck by the raw emotion she saw there – a mixture of shame, regret, and something akin to remorse.

"I... I'm sorry," he mumbled, the words tumbling out in a halting, awkward fashion. "For everything. I didn't mean to."

Janet felt the breath catch in her throat, the weight of his apology both unexpected and profoundly moving. The hurt and anguish she had endured at the hands of her brothers had not been erased, but in this moment, a glimmer of hope began to take root.

Perhaps, she thought, there was a chance for change, for healing and understanding. The journey ahead would not be an easy one, but the small olive branch her brother had extended, however imperfect, gave her the courage to believe that the cycle of cruelty and silence could be broken.

Without a word, Janet nodded, her eyes conveying the depth of her gratitude and the complexity of her emotions. And as she returned to her room, the weight of her past struggles still heavy upon her shoulders, she felt a newfound determination taking shape.

Tomorrow, she would confront her brothers, drawing strength from the experiences that had transformed her on the stage and the support of the friends who had rallied around her. The road ahead would be arduous, but with the determination that now burned bright within her, Janet knew that she was ready to reclaim her voice and her rightful place in the world.

FINDING FORGIVENESS

Janet's eyes fluttered open, the first rays of dawn filtering through her bedroom curtains. Today was different, unlike most mornings when she would linger in bed, consumed by dread and self-doubt. Today, she was filled with a sense of purpose and determination that had been foreign to her for so long.

Sitting up, Janet took a deep, steadying breath, her gaze fixed on her reflection in the mirror across the room. The timid, hunched girl she had once seen staring back at her was gone, replaced by a young woman with a newfound confidence radiating from her very core.

Slowly, she rose from the bed, her movements deliberate and assured. Crossing the room, she opened her closet, her fingers trailing over the familiar fabrics of her wardrobe. After a moment's consideration, she selected a blouse and a pair of slacks – an outfit that spoke of poise and self-assurance, a far cry from the baggy, concealing clothes she had once favored.

As Janet dressed, she found herself standing taller, her shoulders squared and her chin lifted. Catching sight of her reflection once more, she paused, a small smile tugging at the corners of her lips. The person staring back at her was no longer the victim of her brothers' relentless taunts, but a young woman who had found the courage to confront her past and reclaim her voice.

Closing her eyes, Janet took a moment to center herself, drawing strength from the memory of her recent triumph on the stage. The thunderous applause, the validation she had felt – it had ignited a fire within her, a resolve that refused to be extinguished, even in the face of her brothers' cruelty.

A muffled sound from the hallway caught her attention, and Janet felt a familiar twinge of anxiety settle in the pit of her stomach. Her brothers were stirring, their voices carrying a hint of the mockery and disdain that had long defined her existence. But this time, instead of shrinking away, Janet squared her shoulders, her expression hardening with determination.

Today, she would not back down. Today, she would stand her ground and confront the demons that had haunted her for so long. With a deep, steadying breath, Janet made her way towards the door, her steps firm.

The time had come to face her past, to finally give voice to the pain and anguish she had carried for far too long. And this time, she would not be silenced. The familiar sounds of her brothers' voices echoed through the kitchen as Janet descended the stairs, her steps measured and purposeful. Gone was the timid girl.

As Janet entered the room, her brothers' chatter immediately fell silent, their eyes widening in surprise at her confident demeanor. The air was thick with tension, the brothers exchanging puzzled glances, unsure of how to react to this unexpected shift in their sister's behavior.

Squaring her shoulders, Janet met their gaze. "Stop," she said, her voice clear and firm, cutting through the uneasy silence. "I'm done with your constant bullying and insults."

The brothers stared at her, momentarily stunned by her assertiveness. The oldest brother, his brow furrowed, attempted to regain his footing, a mocking grin spreading across his face.

"Well, look who's finally decided to grow a backbone," he sneered, his words dripping with disdain. "What's the matter, Janet? Can't take a little joke?"

But Janet refused to be cowed, her expression hardening as she held her ground. "It's not a joke to me," she replied, her voice steady and resolute. "The way you've treated me – the way you've all treated me – has hurt me, deeply. And I'm not going to let you get away with it anymore."

The room fell silent once more, the brothers' faces shifting from amusement to something akin to discomfort. Janet's youngest brother, his gaze downcast, shifted uncomfortably in his seat, the memory of their late-night encounter weighing heavily upon him.

Clearing his throat, the youngest brother mumbled an unexpected apology, his words barely audible. "I'm sorry," he said, the words tumbling out in a halting, awkward fashion. "I... I didn't mean to, you know, be so awful to you."

The kitchen fell silent, the older brother exchanging bewildered glances, unsure of how to react to this sudden display of contrition. Janet, too, was caught off guard, her brow furrowing as she processed her brother's words.

Seizing the moment of uncertainty, Janet drew a deep, steadying breath, her voice trembling slightly as she began to speak. "For years," she said, her gaze sweeping across the faces of her siblings, "you've all made my life a living hell. The constant taunts, the cruel jokes – it's scarred me in ways you can't even begin to understand."

Janet's heart pounded in her chest, the rush of adrenaline coursing through her veins. She had never before dared to confront her brothers so directly, her fear of their retaliation always holding her back. But now, with the confidence she had discovered on the stage and the support of her new friends, she refused to be silenced.

Maintaining steady eye contact, she continued, her voice unwavering. "I'm tired of being the target of your jokes and cruelty. I'm a person, not just some punching bag for you to take out your frustrations on. And I won't stand for it anymore."

The brothers, with expressions of mixed shame and uncertainty, remained in a state of stunned silence as they processed the weight of Janet's words. For the first time, they were forced to confront the true impact of their actions, the realization that their relentless taunts had inflicted deep, lasting scars upon their sister.

Janet's oldest brother opened his mouth, no doubt ready with a dismissive quip, but she held up a hand, silencing him. "Please, just listen," she implored, her voice steadier than she had expected. "I want you to understand the impact your behavior has had on me."

Janet's voice grew stronger, the weight of her emotions fueling her resolve. "I've spent so much of my life shrinking away, terrified of drawing your attention, of being the target of your ridicule. And it's not fair. I'm a person, with feelings and dreams, and you've all treated me like I'm nothing."

Tears welled in her eyes, but Janet refused to let them fall, her chin held high as she confronted her brothers. "You have no idea the damage you've done," she continued, her words laced with a raw, unyielding honesty. "The way you've made me feel about myself, the way you've chipped away at my confidence – it's been a constant battle just to get through each day. But that ends today. I'm done being the victim, the punching bag for your cruelty. From now on, you're going to listen, and you're going to understand the pain you've caused."

As Janet poured her heart out, she watched the expressions on her brothers' faces shift and change. Flickers of guilt and shame crossed their features, the weight of her words clearly resonating with them in a way it never had before.

Janet's words flowed with a newfound fluency, years of pent-up emotions pouring out. She recounted specific incidents from their childhood, moments where their cruel laughter and relentless ridicule had chipped away at her self-worth, leaving deep scars that still ached.

Her brothers sat in stunned silence, their expressions shifting from discomfort to a dawning realization. Flickers of guilt and shame crossed their features as they began to comprehend the full extent of the pain they had inflicted.

Janet's voice grew stronger with each passing moment, her eyes shining with a mix of vulnerability and conviction. This was no longer the timid, insecure girl they had once known – this was a young woman who had found the courage to confront her demons, to stand up for herself in a way she had never dared before.

The room was thick with tension as the siblings confronted their shared history, the air thick with the weight of unspoken emotions. Janet could feel her heart pounding in her chest, but she refused to back down, determined to give voice to the pain that had long been silenced. As Janet's words hung heavy in the air, her oldest brother shifted uncomfortably, his expression shifting from guilt to a familiar mask of bravado.

"Aw, come on, sis," he scoffed, attempting to deflect with a forced chuckle. "You're blowing this way out of proportion. We were just messing around, you know that. Can't you take a joke?"

But Janet refused to be swayed, her gaze firm as she held her ground. "No," she said, her voice also firm and unyielding. "This isn't a joke to me. The way you've treated me, the way you've made me feel – it's been anything but funny."

The oldest brother's smile faltered, his eyes darting away from Janet's intense stare. The other brother, too, shifted uncomfortably in his seat, the realization that their actions had truly hurt their sister beginning to sink in.

But Janet refused to be swayed, her gaze unwavering as she met his eyes. "Your 'messing around' has had a real impact on me, and I won't let you minimize that anymore."

The tension in the room ratcheted up as the siblings confronted each other, the air thick with years of unresolved resentment. Janet could feel her heart pounding in her chest, but she refused to back down, determined to be heard.

Suddenly, her youngest brother, who had been uncharacteristically silent, shifted in his seat, his expression a mix of discomfort and remorse.

"I'm... I'm sorry, Janet," he mumbled, his words barely audible. "I remember that night, when we... when I..." He trailed off, his gaze dropping to the floor.

The unexpected apology created a momentary pause in the confrontation, the air thick with a fragile vulnerability. Janet felt a flicker of surprise crossed her features, her anger momentarily tempered by the glimmer of genuine remorse in her brother's eyes.

For a heartbeat, the siblings sat in a charged silence, the weight of their shared history palpable. Janet could feel the walls she had so carefully built beginning to crumble, a glimmer of hope emerging amidst the turmoil. Emboldened by the unexpected gesture from her youngest brother, Janet pressed on, her voice growing stronger as she continued to express the depth of her pain.

She recounted specific incidents from their childhood, moments where their cruel taunts and relentless ridicule had cut her to the core. The time they had mocked her in front of her classmates, leaving her humiliated and ashamed. The night they had cornered her in the hallway, their laughter echoing like a haunting melody.

"You have no idea what it's been like," she said, her words laced with a raw, unfiltered honesty. "To constantly live in fear of your taunts, to dread coming home because I know I'll be the target of your ridicule."

The brothers remained silent, their expressions shifting from defiance to something akin to shame. The oldest brother, his bravado fading, opened his mouth as if to speak, but quickly closed it, his gaze downcast.

In that moment, Janet felt a surge of empowerment coursing through her. She had found her voice, and she was determined to use it, no matter the consequences. The time for silence and submission had passed – now, it was the time to confront the demons of her past, once and for all.

As Janet continued to pour her heart out, the conversation in the room quickly escalated, the air thick with years of pent-up emotions and resentment. She took advantage of the opportunity, her eyes sweeping across her siblings' faces. "For years," she continued, "you've made me feel like I'm worthless, like I'm nothing more than your punching bag for your own insecurities. But I'm not going to let you do that anymore."

Her brothers, confronted with the stark reality of their cruelty, struggled to defend themselves and began to truly listen. The oldest brother, his expression shifting from amusement to discomfort, attempted to interject, but Janet refused to be silenced.

Janet could see the realization dawning on them, the understanding that their cruel behavior had inflicted deep, lasting scars upon their sister.

The oldest brother opened his mouth again, no doubt ready with another dismissive quip, but the words died on his lips. He exchanged a troubled glance with his sibling, the bravado that had once shielded them now crumbling in the face of Janet's raw honesty.

Janet's voice trembled with emotion, the pain she had long suppressed now pouring out in a torrent of words. The brothers struggled to defend themselves, their usual retorts and excuses failing them. They sat in stunned silence, their expressions shifting from discomfort to a dawning realization of the harm they had inflicted.

In that moment, Janet could see the facade they had so carefully maintained begin to crumble. The brothers, once so quick to ridicule and taunt, now appeared vulnerable and uncertain, grappling with the weight of their actions. The conversation reached a crescendo as years of pent-up emotions surged to the surface. Janet's voice trembled with raw vulnerability as she recounted the pain and insecurity her brothers' bullying had caused.

Tears flowed freely down her cheeks as she described the countless nights she had spent lying awake, tormented by their cruel laughter and the relentless barrage of insults. The way their taunts had chipped away at her self-worth, leaving her feeling unworthy and alone. Occasional glances at the family photos scattered around the room served as stark reminders of happier times – a painful juxtaposition to the raw, anguished exchange unfolding before them.

Janet's voice grew stronger, her words laced with a lifetime of repressed frustration and resentment. She described the way their bullying had made her feel, the way it had robbed her of her confidence and her sense of self.

The room was thick with tension, the air charged with the weight of unspoken emotions. Janet could feel her heart pounding in her chest, but she still refused to back down, determined to give voice to the pain that had long been In the midst of the intense exchange, the sound of footsteps in the hallway drew the siblings' attention. Janet's parents, alarmed by the commotion, entered the room, their expressions etched with concern.

Janet, caught up in the raw emotion of the moment, continued to stand her ground, her voice firm as she poured out the depth of her pain and resentment. But as her parents took in the scene before them, their faces shifting from confusion to shock, a temporary pause settled over the confrontation.

Janet's mother, her eyes brimming with tears, moved towards her daughter, a trembling hand reaching out to gently touch her arm.

"Janet, what's going on?" she asked, her voice thick with emotion. "What... what have you all been doing to your sister?"

The brothers exchanged guilty glances, their expressions shifting as they were confronted with the full weight of their parents' dismay. Janet's father, his brow furrowed with a mixture of anger and disbelief, turned to his sons, demanding an explanation.

"Enough," he said, his voice firm but tinged with a hint of sorrow. The room fell silent, the brothers shifting uncomfortably as their parents' gaze swept across them.

"I can't believe this," his voice laced with a rare intensity. "All this time, and we had no idea the extent of what you've been doing to your own sister?"

The siblings fell silent, the air thick with tension as the family dynamics shifted. Janet, with her heart still pounding, felt a surge of both relief and trepidation as her parents' presence created a temporary pause in the confrontation.

She knew that this was a pivotal moment, a chance for her family to finally confront the toxic patterns that had taken root over the years. And as her parents' expressions shifted from shock to a deep, profound sorrow, Janet steeled herself, prepared to continue the difficult but necessary dialogue. With their parents now present, the family discussion shifted into a raw, honest dialogue about their relationships and the toxic patterns that had developed over the years.

Janet's mother, her eyes brimming with tears, moved closer to her daughter, a trembling hand reaching out to her.

"Oh, Janet," she breathed, her voice thick with emotion. "I had no idea... I should have seen what was happening, I should have done something."

Her father, his expression a mix of anger and profound sorrow, turned to his sons, his gaze piercing.

"Explain yourselves," he demanded, his voice laced with an intensity that was uncharacteristic of the usually mild-mannered man. "How could you do this to your own sister?"

The brothers, confronted with the weight of their cruelty, attempted to deflect and minimize their behavior, but Janet refused to let them off the hook. "No," she insisted, her eyes blazing with a newfound determination. "You don't get to pretend this didn't happen. You need to own up to what you've done, to the pain you've caused."

As the family confronted the painful truths that had long been buried, the air in the room grew heavy with emotion. Janet watched as the carefully constructed walls of her parents' composure began to crack, their expressions shifting from shock to a profound sorrow.

This was no longer a confrontation between siblings, but a raw, honest dialogue about the complex web of relationships and unaddressed issues that had taken root within the family. Years of unspoken resentment, guilt, and pain bubbled to the surface, the facade of their perfect family life crumbling before their eyes.

The parents, their hearts heavy with the realization of their own failures, interjected; their voices tinged with a desperate plea for understanding. "We should have seen the signs, should have done more to protect you, Janet," the mother said, her gaze sweeping across the siblings. "But we're here now, and we're going to make this right."

The father, his expression hardening with resolve, turned to the brothers, his voice firm and unyielding. "You will apologize to your sister," he said, leaving no room for argument. "And then, we're going to have a long, hard conversation about the dynamics in this family and how we're going to move forward."

Janet felt a mix of relief and trepidation as the conversation unfolded. She knew that this was a necessary step, a chance for her family to finally confront the toxic patterns that had shaped their lives. But the vulnerability and uncertainty of it all weighed heavily on her heart, as she braced herself for the difficult journey that lay ahead. As the intensity of the confrontation began to wane, a fragile silence settled over the room. The family, emotionally drained from the raw exchange, seemed to collectively hold their breath, the air thick with unspoken emotions.

In the midst of this charged stillness, Janet's oldest brother shifted in his seat. All eyes turned to him as he cleared his throat, his expression a mix of discomfort and genuine remorse.

"I... I'm sorry," he began, his voice barely above a whisper. "I know that doesn't make up for what I've done, but... I want you to know that a lot of it was because of my own insecurities."

The admission hung in the air, creating a palpable shift in the atmosphere. Janet felt a flicker of surprise, her anger and resentment momentarily tempered by the unexpected vulnerability of her brother's words.

He went on to explain how his own struggles with self-esteem had contributed to his need to assert dominance, to find some way to feel superior amidst the chaos of adolescence. The guilt and shame that had long festered within him now bubbled to the surface, his expression etched with a raw honesty that caught the family off guard.

As he spoke, the siblings exchanged glances, the tension in the room slowly giving way to a fragile understanding. The walls that had once divided them began to fall, replaced by a willingness to listen, to empathize, and to confront the complex web of emotions that had shaped their relationships.

In that moment, Janet felt a glimmer of hope take root in her heart. Perhaps, through this unexpected vulnerability and the opening of honest communication, the path towards healing and reconciliation might finally begin to emerge. As the fragile silence settled over the room, the family discussion gradually evolved into a tentative exploration of how to move forward. Janet, drawing on the insights she had gained through her transformative journey in the theater, began to suggest ways they could improve their communication and support one another.

Her voice, once trembling with emotion, now carried a newfound steadiness and conviction. She spoke of the importance of open and honest dialogue, of creating a safe space where each family member could express their feelings without fear of judgment or ridicule.

Her brothers, still visibly processing the weight of their guilt, exchanged cautious glances before offering their own ideas for making amends. The eldest brother, his expression etched with remorse, acknowledged the need to take accountability for his actions and find ways to rebuild the trust he had shattered.

Their parents, having witnessed the raw intensity of the confrontation and the depth of the family's unresolved issues, recognized the need for a more comprehensive approach to healing. Janet's father, his brow furrowed with a mix of concern and determination, proposed the idea of family counseling – a chance for them to work through their conflicts and rebuild the foundation of their relationships.

As the discussion unfolded, the family members gradually found themselves on more stable footing, the initial tension and defensiveness giving way to a fragile sense of hope. Though the path ahead was uncertain, there was a palpable shift in the atmosphere, a growing recognition that by confronting their challenges head-on, they might finally find a way to mend the fractures that had long divided them.

Janet listened intently, her heart swelling with a mix of confusion and cautious optimism. She knew that the journey towards reconciliation would not be an easy one, but in this moment, she felt a sense of purpose and determination – a belief that by working together, her family could emerge from the shadows of their past and forge a brighter future. As the evening drew to a close, a palpable change had settled over the family. The raw intensity of the confrontation had given way to a fragile sense of relief, the air thick with the weight of their shared history and the uncertainty of the path that lay ahead.

One by one, the family members began to disperse, the tension gradually dissipating as they each retreated to their own corners of the house. Janet's parents exchanged a weighty glance, their expressions etched with a mix of sorrow and determination, before quietly exiting the room.

And then, to Janet's surprise, her oldest brother approached her, his movements uncharacteristically tentative and awkward.

"Hey, uh, Janet," he began, his gaze shifting nervously. "I was wondering if... if you might need some help with that school project you've been working on."

The unexpected gesture caught Janet off guard, a flicker of surprise crossing her features. For years, her brother had been the ring-leader of the taunts and jeers, the one who had inflicted the deepest wounds. But now, in the wake of their raw and emotional confrontation, there was a glimmer of vulnerability in his expression, a small but significant step towards reconciliation.

Janet nodded slowly, her own exhaustion and uncertainty warring with a sense of cautious hope. "Yeah, that... that would be great," she replied, her voice barely above a whisper.

As her brother offered a stilted nod and turned to leave, Janet felt a mix of emotions wash over her. The evening had been a tumultuous one, a rollercoaster of pain, resentment, and the tentative beginnings of understanding. And as she headed towards her room, she couldn't help but feel a profound sense of both exhaustion and hope.

This conversation, as difficult and draining as it had been, was just the beginning of a long and challenging journey towards healing. The path ahead was uncertain, fraught with the potential for further conflict and the daunting task of rebuilding trust and understanding. But in this moment, Janet felt a glimmer of determination take root within her – a belief that, with time and effort, her family might just find a way to mend the fractures that had long divided them.

EMBRACING THE SPOTLIGHT

Janet stood at the entrance of the theater, her heart pounding with a mix of excitement and trepidation. After weeks of anticipation and self-doubt, she had finally arrived for her first rehearsal as part of the cast. Taking a deep, steadying breath, she stepped through the doors, her senses immediately enveloped by the bustling energy of the space.

New actors of all ages were scattered throughout the room, some warming up their voices with vocal exercises, others huddled together, running lines and gesturing animatedly. The air was charged with a palpable sense of creativity and camaraderie, and Janet felt a surge of awe wash over her. She was now a part of this vibrant, artistic community – a realization that both thrilled and overwhelmed her.

As she made her way across the stage, her eyes darted around, taking in every detail. The polished wooden floor, the towering backdrop, the rows of empty seats in the audience – it was all so different from the quiet, familiar confines of her high school. She felt like a small fish in a vast, captivating ocean, unsure of where to focus her gaze.

Suddenly, the warm, friendly voice cut through the din, drawing Janet's attention. "Hi Janet! Welcome to the team."

Janet turned to see a woman with kind eyes and a gentle smile approaching her. Straightening her posture, she offered a tentative smile in return. It was Maria, the director.

Maria chuckled softly, placing a reassuring hand on Janet's shoulder. "No need to be nervous, dear. We're so glad to have you here." Janet notices new faces. Turning to the rest of the cast, Maria gestured towards Janet. "Everyone, this is Janet, our newest addition to our cast. Let's make her feel right at home."

A chorus of enthusiastic greetings and welcoming smiles washed over Janet, her cheeks flushing with a mix of surprise and gratitude. As the other actors introduced themselves, she struggled to keep up with the flurry of names and faces, her mind whirling with the sheer magnitude of the experience.

When the director called for the first rehearsal to begin, Janet took her place alongside the rest of the cast, her palms sweating and her heart racing. As the director began to outline the expectations and terminology of the theater world, Janet was both captivated and overwhelmed, her head spinning with unfamiliar terms and concepts.

Yet, despite the initial disorientation, a spark of excitement began to ignite within her. This was her chance, her opportunity to step out of the shadows and into the spotlight, to shed the insecurities that had defined her for so long. With a deep, steadying breath, Janet steeled her resolve, determined to embrace the challenges that lay ahead.

As the rehearsal progressed, she swept up in the energy and camaraderie of the group, her initial trepidation slowly giving way to a growing sense of belonging. The director's guidance and the supportive encouragement of her castmates helped to ease her nerves, and Janet began to find her footing, her movements and delivery becoming more natural with each passing moment.

By the time the rehearsal drew to a close, Janet felt a profound sense of accomplishment. She had taken the first step on a journey of self-discovery, and though the road ahead was uncertain, she knew that she was no longer alone. Surrounded by this vibrant, accepting community, she felt a glimmer of hope taking root.

The next rehearsal began with a scene study exercise, and Janet was paired with a confident, outgoing actress named Zoe. As they took their places on the stage, Janet felt a familiar flutter of nerves in the pit of her stomach.

When the director called for them to begin, Janet stumbled over her lines, her voice trembling with uncertainty. Immediately, she felt the heat of embarrassment rise to her cheeks as she stammered out an apology.

But to Janet's surprise, Zoe simply offered her a warm smile. "No need to apologize," she said, her tone gentle and encouraging. "We all have those moments when the words just don't want to come out right."

Zoe then proceeded to share her own experiences of struggling with stage fright during her early days in the theater. Her openness and willingness to be vulnerable caught Janet off guard, and she felt the tension in her shoulders begin to ease.

Emboldened by Zoe's kindness, she took a deep breath and tried the scene again. This time, her delivery was more natural, the words flowing with greater ease as she allowed herself to get lost in the moment.

As they continued to work through the lines, Zoe offered subtle tips and encouragement, guiding Janet with a deft touch. The director, observing their progress, nodded approvingly, a small smile tugging at the corners of her lips.

When the exercise concluded, the director stepped forward, her gaze settling on Janet. "Wonderful work, both of you," she said, her voice warm and sincere. "Janet, I'm particularly impressed by the way you've opened up and embraced the character. Keep it up, and you'll be shining on that stage in no time."

Janet felt a surge of pride and accomplishment wash over her. She had come so far from the timid, self-conscious girl who had first stepped into the theater, and in that moment, she knew that this was only the beginning of her transformative journey.

As the rehearsal continued, Janet felt more at ease, her movements and delivery becoming more fluid with each passing exercise. The support and encouragement of her castmates, coupled with the director's guidance, had helped to chip away at the walls she had built up over the years, allowing her true self to shine through.

By the time the rehearsal drew to a close, Janet felt a profound sense of belonging and purpose. This vibrant, accepting community had become a safe haven, a place where she could explore her passions and discover the full breadth of her capabilities. And with each passing day, she could feel the weight of her insecurities slowly beginning to lift, replaced by a growing sense of self-assurance and determination. As the rehearsal came to a close, Janet hesitated by the edge of the stage, unsure of where to go during the lunch break. The familiar feeling of self-consciousness crept back in, and she was reluctant to join the rest of the cast.

But before she could retreat, a warm voice called out to her. "Hey, Janet! Care to join us for lunch?" The invitation came from Zoe, the actress she had worked with earlier, her expression open and friendly.

Janet felt her heart skip a beat, both surprised and touched by the gesture. Swallowing the lump in her throat, she nodded tentatively and followed Zoe to a group of cast members gathered in the corner of the theater.

As she approached, the others turned to greet her, their faces alight with welcoming smiles. "Come on, sit with us," one of the actors said, gesturing to an empty spot in their circle. We were just about to dig in.

Feeling a mix of trepidation and curiosity, Janet lowered herself onto the floor, her gaze darting between the unfamiliar faces. To her surprise, the others immediately began to engage her in conversation, asking about her background and previous experience with theater.

Hesitantly, Janet started opening up, sharing the story of how she had mustered the courage to audition, despite her overwhelming fears and self-doubts. As she spoke, she was met with genuine admiration and support, the others nodding emphatically and offering words of encouragement.

"I can't believe you had the guts to just go for it," one of the actresses exclaimed, her eyes wide with wonder. "That's so inspiring!"

Another cast member chimed in, his expression earnest. "Yeah, I remember being a total mess when I first started out. But you've got something special, Janet. I can see it."

The warmth and acceptance radiating from the group enveloped Janet, and she felt a profound sense of belonging.. These were her peers now, her fellow artists, united by a shared passion for the theater – and they had welcomed her with open arms.

As the conversation continued, Janet started to relax, her initial hesitation slowly melting away. She listened intently as the others shared their own stories, their words painting a vivid picture of the challenges and triumphs they had faced on their journeys.

Janet didn't feel like an outsider, a shy and insecure girl clinging to the shadows. Here, she was seen, she was heard, and she was valued – not in spite of her vulnerabilities, but because of them.

When the lunch break drew to a close, Janet rose to her feet, her steps lighter and her spirit buoyed by the newfound sense of camaraderie. As she made her way back to the stage, she couldn't help but marvel at the transformation she had undergone in such a short span of time.

This theater, this community – it had become a sanctuary, a place where she could shed the weight of her insecurities and embrace the full breadth of her potential. And with each passing day, she could feel the walls she had built up over the years slowly crumbling, being replaced by a growing sense of confidence and self-acceptance. The character Janet was portraying captivated her, and she was getting more and more emotionally attached to her character as the rehearsals progressed.

 The director had assigned the cast a particularly poignant scene, one that required them to tap into their own experiences of pain and vulnerability.

When it came time for Janet's turn, she felt a familiar flutter of nerves in the pit of her stomach. But this time, instead of shrinking away, she took a deep, steadying breath and allowed the emotions to wash over her.

As she delivered her lines, Janet was drawn upon the memories of her own struggles – the taunts, the insecurities, the overwhelming sense of inadequacy that had once defined her. The words spilled forth, laced with a raw, unfiltered honesty that seemed to reverberate through the space.

Tears began to stream down her face, and Janet felt a profound sense of catharsis wash over her. It was as if she were shedding the weight of her past, each syllable a witness to the journey she had undertaken to find her voice.

The director called "cut," and for a moment, the theater fell silent, the cast members staring at Janet with a mixture of awe and reverence. Then, the room erupted in thunderous applause, the sound of their hands clapping filling the air.

Janet, overwhelmed by the response, felt a surge of emotions coursing through her. She had always viewed her vulnerability as a weakness, a liability that needed to be hidden away. But in this moment, she realized that it had become her greatest strength – a wellspring of authenticity and raw power that had captivated her audience.

As the applause died down, the director approached Janet, her eyes glistening with unshed tears. "That was truly remarkable," she said, her voice thick with emotion. "The depth of feeling you brought to that scene – it was breathtaking."

Janet felt a flush of pride and disbelief wash over her. She had always been the shy, insecure girl, the one who shrank away from the spotlight. But here she was, standing tall and confident, her vulnerability now a source of strength rather than weakness.

The other cast members gathered around her, offering words of praise and admiration. "You were amazing, Janet," one of the actresses said, her eyes shining with genuine respect. "I've never seen anything like it."

In that moment, Janet felt a profound sense of belonging and acceptance. These were her peers, her fellow artists, and they had recognized the power of her performance, the authenticity that had poured forth from the depths of her soul.

As the rehearsal continued, Janet found herself more at ease, her movements and delivery imbued with confidence. She no longer feared her own vulnerability, but rather, embraced it as a tool to bring depth and nuance to her character.

The director's praise and the enthusiastic support of her castmates had ignited a fire within her, fueling her determination to continue exploring the transformative power of the theater. And with each passing day, Janet could feel the walls she had built up over the years were slowly crumbling down, replaced by a growing sense of self-acceptance and the courage to be her authentic self. As the rehearsals continued, Janet couldn't help but notice a gradual change in her own posture and demeanor. Gone was the timid, hunched figure she had once been, replaced by a young woman who stood taller, her gaze more direct and her movements more assured than ever before.

During the scene work, she noticed she was making eye contact with her castmates more easily, her voice projecting with a newfound confidence that surprised even her. The transformation was subtle, but undeniable, and it didn't go unnoticed by the others.

"You know, Janet," one of the actresses remarked during a break, "your presence on stage has really blossomed. There's a certain poise and confidence about you now that's just captivating to watch." Janet felt a flush of pride and disbelief wash over her. But now, here she was, being praised for the very qualities she had once tried to suppress for so many years.

Another cast member chimed in, his expression warm and sincere. "Absolutely. You really seem to have found your footing, both on stage and off. It's inspiring to see, you know?"

As the rehearsals progressed, Janet couldn't help but reflect on the profound changes she had undergone. The theater, this vibrant community of artists, this sanctuary is where she could shed the weight of her insecurities and embrace the full breadth of her potential.

Gone were the days when she would hunch her shoulders and avoid eye contact, desperate to make herself as small and inconspicuous as possible. Now, she carried herself with a sense of purpose and self-assurance, her movements fluid and her voice steady.

This transformation wasn't limited to the stage, either. Janet became more assertive in other areas of her life, no longer willing to shrink away from challenges or let her fears hold her back. The confidence she had discovered through her theater experience had seeped into every aspect of her existence, empowering her to take risks and embrace her true self.

Her castmates continued to comment on the change, their words confirming the profound impact the theater had had on Janet's self-perception. "You're really blossoming," one of the actresses said, her eyes shining with genuine admiration. "It's amazing to witness."

Janet couldn't help but smile, her heart swelling with a sense of pride and gratitude. This theater, this community, had become a catalyst for her transformation, a safe haven where she could explore the depths of her own creativity.

Janet was no longer just a passive observer, but an active participant in the creative process, her voice and her presence integral to the success of the production. And with each passing day, she could feel the weight of her insecurities slowly lifting off and being replaced by a confidence and self-assurance that radiated from every fiber of her being. The theater had become like a mirror, reflecting back to her the strength and beauty she had always possessed, but had been too afraid to embrace.

As the rehearsals pressed on, Janet encountered a particularly challenging moment during a scene that required her to deliver a complex monologue. Try as she might, she stumbled over the lines, her frustration mounting with each flubbed delivery.

The director called for a break, and Janet retreated to the edge of the stage, her brow furrowed in concentration as she pored over the script, desperate to get the words right. But no matter how many times she ran through the lines, they refused to stick, her mind a whirlwind of self-doubt and insecurity.

Just as she was about to give up, a familiar face appeared in her periphery. Liam, the kind-hearted classmate who had encouraged her to audition in the first place, approached with a gentle smile.

"Hey, you've got this, Janet," he said, his voice soft and reassuring. "I know it's tough, but I believe in you. You've come so far, and I'm not about to let you give up now."

Janet felt a surge of gratitude and determination wash over her. Liam's support had been a constant throughout her journey, a steadfast anchor that had helped her weather the storms of self-doubt and fear.

Squaring her shoulders, she took a deep, steadying breath and approached the director. "Can I try that monologue one more time?" she asked, her voice laced with a newfound resolve.

The director, sensing the shift in Janet's demeanor, nodded and gestured for her to take her place. As Janet stepped into the spotlight, she felt a familiar flutter of nerves, but this time, she refused to let them consume her.

Closing her eyes for a moment, she drew upon the well of emotions she had tapped into during the earlier rehearsals – the pain, the insecurity, the resilience that had become the very foundation of her transformation. And when she opened her mouth to speak, the words flowed forth with a raw, unfiltered honesty that seemed to captivate the entire room.

As she delivered the monologue, she poured her heart into every syllable, her movements and expression imbued with a depth and authenticity that left the director and her castmates spellbound. When she finished, the theater fell silent, the air thick with a palpable tension.

Then, the director stepped forward, her eyes glistening with unshed tears. "Janet," she said, her voice thick with emotion, "that was truly remarkable. The resilience and growth you've shown — it's nothing short of inspiring."

The cast erupted into thunderous applause, their cheers and accolades washing over Janet like a tidal wave of validation and support. In that moment, she knew that she had found her voice, not just on the stage, but within the very depths of her being.

As the rehearsal continued, Janet felt a sense of confidence and determination coursing through her veins. The challenges that had once seemed insurmountable now felt like opportunities to showcase her hard-won skills and resilience.

And with each passing day, she could feel the transformation taking root, her posture and demeanor growing more assured, her movements and delivery more fluid and expressive. The theater had become a crucible, forging her into the confident, self-assured young woman she had always had the potential to be.

As the opening night of the production drew closer, Janet felt a familiar flutter of anxiety begin to resurface. The progress she had made, the newfound confidence she had discovered — it all seemed to fade away, replaced by a crippling self-doubt that threatened to consume her.

During a crucial dress rehearsal, the moment of truth arrived. As Janet stepped onto the stage, her lines suddenly fled her mind, leaving her frozen and overwhelmed. The director called cut, and the theater fell silent, the weight of Janet's struggle palpable in the air.

But before she could spiral further into despair, her castmates sprang into action, surrounding her with an outpouring of support and understanding. One by one, they shared their own stories of battling stage fright.

"I remember my first opening night," one of the more experienced performers said, her expression empathetic. "I was a nervous wreck, my hands shaking so badly I could barely hold my script."

Another chimed in, his tone reassuring. "And me? I used to have these awful panic attacks before every single show. Thought I was going to pass out on stage."

As the cast members shared their personal experiences, she felt a wave of relief over her. She wasn't alone in her struggle – these were her peers, her theater family, and they understood the depths of the fear and self-doubt that threatened to consume her.

Buoyed by their support, she listened intently as the cast members offered practical coping strategies, from deep breathing exercises to visualization techniques. With each word of encouragement, she felt the tension in her shoulders begin to ease, the weight of her anxiety slowly lifting.

Summoning her courage, Janet took a deep breath and asked to try the scene again. This time, as she delivered her lines, she could feel the raw emotion and authenticity infusing her performance, the support of her castmates giving her the strength to push through her fear.

When the rehearsal drew to a close, the director approached Janet, a warm smile spreading across her face. "Wonderful work," she said, her voice filled with genuine pride. "You should be incredibly proud of yourself."

Janet felt a surge of gratitude and accomplishment wash over her. She had faced her demons head-on once more, and with the support of her theater family, she had emerged even stronger and more resilient than ever before.

As the cast gathered for a post-rehearsal debrief, was surrounded by a chorus of congratulations and heartfelt embraces. The sense of camaraderie and acceptance she felt in that moment was unlike anything she had ever experienced, a testament to the transformative power of this vibrant, supportive community.

In the days leading up to opening night, Janet's anxiety continued to ebb and flow, but she now had an arsenal of coping strategies and the support of her castmates to draw upon. And as she stepped onto the stage, even with her heart pounding with a mix of nerves and exhilaration, she knew that she was no longer alone in her journey.

And with each performance, she could feel the last vestiges of her self-doubt melting away, replaced by a growing sense of confidence and self-assurance that radiated from every fiber of her being. As the final dress rehearsal drew to a close, the cast gathered in a circle, preparing to engage in a cherished pre-show ritual. Janet stood among them, her heart swelling with a mix of anticipation and trepidation.

When the director called for them to join hands, Janet felt a familiar warmth envelop her. Glancing around the circle, she was struck by how much she had changed since first stepping into the theater.

As the cast members began to share words of encouragement and support, Janet felt a lump rise in her throat. This wasn't just a group of performers – they had become her family, a community that had embraced her with open arms and nurtured her transformation.

When it was her turn to speak, Janet surprised even herself with the eloquence of her words. "I... I don't even know where to begin," she began, her voice trembling slightly. "When I first walked through those doors, I was terrified, convinced that I didn't belong here. But you all – you welcomed me, supported me, and believed in me, even when I couldn't believe in myself."

Tears welled in her eyes as she continued, her gaze sweeping across the faces of her castmates. "This theater, this family – you've changed me in ways I never thought possible. I'm not just playing a role on stage; I'm discovering my true self, the person I was always meant to be."

Several of the cast members had tears streaming down their cheeks. She had come so far, from a shy, insecure girl to a confident, self-assured young woman, and they had all borne witness to her remarkable journey.

"Thank you," Janet said, her voice thick with emotion. "Thank you for your support, your encouragement, and your belief in me. I wouldn't be here without all of you, and I'll be forever grateful for the gift you've given me."

As the cast members erupted into a cheer, breaking the circle with a resounding energy, Janet felt a sense of readiness and purpose wash over her. She was no longer just an actor, a performer – she was a storyteller, a vessel for the emotions and experiences that had once defined her.

And as she stepped out onto the stage, ready to face the audience, Janet knew that she had found her voice, her place in this vibrant, accepting community. The insecurities that had once held her back were now a distant memory, replaced by a deep well of confidence and self-assurance that radiated from every fiber of her being.

This was her moment, her chance to share her journey, her transformation, with the world. And as the curtain rose, Janet took a deep breath, her gaze filled with a determination that refused to be extinguished. She was ready, more ready than she had ever been before, to embrace the spotlight and let her true self shine.

RECLAIMING HER VOICE

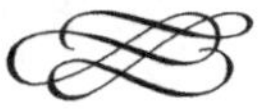

Janet strode through the school's main entrance, her steps purposeful and her head held high. Gone was the timid, hunched figure that had once been her constant companion. In her place stood a young woman brimming with newfound confidence, the weight of her insecurities no longer weighing her down.

As she passed her brothers in the hallway, Janet met their gaze directly, refusing to shrink away from their scrutiny. The surprise that flashed across their faces only fueled her determination. She was no longer the meek, easily-cowed sibling they had once tormented; she had found her voice, and she was ready to use it.

Spotting Liam in the distance, Janet felt a smile spread across her face. He had been a constant source of encouragement and support throughout her transformative journey, and she couldn't wait to share her recent triumph with him.

Quickening her pace, Janet approached Liam, her expression radiating with self-assurance. "Hey, Liam," she greeted, her voice clear and steady. "You'll never guess what happened at home last night."

Liam's face lit up with a warm smile, his eyes reflecting the pride he felt for his friend's progress. "I'm all ears," he replied, his tone encouraging.

Janet took a deep breath, the memory of her confrontation with her brothers still fresh in her mind. "I finally stood up to them," she began, her words laced with a mixture of triumph and relief. "I looked them straight in the eye and told them to stop their constant taunting. And you know what? They actually listened."

Liam's eyes widened with genuine admiration. "That's amazing, Janet," he exclaimed, reaching out to give her shoulder a supportive squeeze. "I knew you had it in you. I'm so proud of you."

Janet felt a surge of gratitude wash over her. Liam's belief in her had been a driving force behind her transformation, and in this moment, she knew that she had made the right decision to step out of the shadows and embrace her true self.

"It wasn't easy," she admitted, her gaze momentarily drifting to the floor before meeting Liam's once more. "But I realized that I'm done hiding, done being the timid, insecure girl they've always known. I'm ready to be seen, Liam. I'm ready to use my voice."

Liam nodded, his expression filled with understanding. "And you should be proud of that, Janet," he said, his voice warm and sincere. "You've come so far, and I know this is just the beginning of an incredible journey."

As the bell rang, signaling the start of the school day, Janet felt a renewed sense of purpose coursing through her veins. With her head held high and her shoulders squared, she made her way to her first class, her steps lighter and her spirit buoyed by the knowl-edge that she was no longer alone in her quest for self-discovery. As Janet settled into her seat, the familiar flutter of nerves she had once felt began to dissipate, replaced by a growing sense of confidence and determination. When the teacher called on her to answer a question, Janet raised her her hand without a moment's hesitation.

Her classmates turned to look at her, some with surprise etched on their faces, others with respect shining in their eyes. Janet's voice rang out, clear and steady, as she delivered her response, the words flowing with a natural ease that she had once struggled to find.

The teacher's expression shifted from mild curiosity to one of genuine admiration. "Excellent, Janet," she praised, her tone warm and encouraging. "That was a thoughtful and insightful contribution."

Janet felt a surge of pride swell within her, the teacher's words like a balm to her once-fragile self-esteem. Across the room, she caught Liam's gaze, and the encouraging grin that spread across his face only served to bolster her sense of accomplishment.

Gone were the days when Janet would have shrunk away, her voice barely audible, her body language conveying a deep-seated insecu-rity. Now, she sat tall, her posture exuding a quiet confidence that had once seemed so elusive.

As the lesson continued, Janet started participating actively, her hand raised on multiple occasions as she shared her thoughts and insights. Each time, her classmates turned to her with a newfound respect, their expressions reflecting a growing appreciation for the transformation they were witnessing.

Janet could feel the weight of her past insecurities slowly lifting while being replaced by a sense of empowerment and self-assurance that radiated from every fiber of her being. This was her moment to shine, to show the world that she was no longer the timid, easily-overlooked girl they had once known.

And with each passing minute, Janet could feel the last vestiges of her self-doubt melting away, replaced by a deep well of determination and resilience. She was in control of her own narrative now, and she was ready to let her voice be heard. As the lunch bell rang, Janet made her way to the cafeteria. Spotting her theater friends gathered in the corner, she approached them with a warm smile, eager to join their animated discussion about the upcoming production.

Janet listened intently as the group shared their ideas and concerns, her voice chiming in with thoughtful contributions that showcased her growing confidence and understanding of the creative process.

But just as Janet was fully immersed in the conversation, a familiar and unwelcome presence caught her attention. Her brothers, passing by, made a snide comment under their breath, their words laced with the same taunting tone she had endured for years.

Without hesitation, Janet rose from her seat and looked directly at her brothers without flinching. The cafeteria fell silent, all eyes drawn to the unexpected confrontation.

"Stop," Janet said, her voice calm but firm. "I'm not going to let you keep belittling me. Not anymore."

Her brothers, caught off guard by her assertiveness, shifted uncomfortably, their expressions a mix of surprise and discomfort. They mumbled a half-hearted response before quickly retreating, the weight of Janet's words and the scrutiny of the onlookers too much for them to bear.

The cafeteria remained hushed for a moment, the tension palpable in the air. Then, one by one, Janet's theater friends began to applaud, their faces alight with admiration and respect. Janet felt a surge of pride and accomplishment wash over her, the magnitude of her transformation finally sinking in.

No longer was she the shy, easily-cowed girl her brothers had once known. In her place stood a young woman who had found the courage to stand up for herself, to reclaim her voice and assert her rightful place in the world.

As Janet returned to her seat, her theater friends gathered around her, offering words of praise and encouragement. "That was amazing, Janet," one of them exclaimed, her eyes shining with genuine admiration. "I can't believe you just did that."

Janet felt a flush of pride spread across her cheeks, but this time, it was not born of embarrassment or self-consciousness. Rather, it was a testament to the strength and resilience she had discovered within herself, a sense of self-worth that refused to be diminished by the taunts and jeers of others.

In that moment, Janet knew that she had taken a monumental step forward in her journey of self-discovery. As the afternoon wore on, Janet made her way through the bustling school hallways, her steps lighter and her spirit buoyed by the events of the day. The confrontation with her brothers had been a pivotal moment, a confirmation to the strength and resilience she had within herself.

But as Janet turned the corner, her gaze fell upon a sight that immediately stirred her empathy and concern. A group of older students were surrounding a younger peer, their taunts and jeers echoing through the corridor. The victim, a small, timid-looking individual, cowered under the weight of the bullies' relentless assault.

Without a moment's hesitation, Janet felt a surge of determination course through her veins. Drawing on her own experiences of being the target of such cruelty, she strode forward, her posture exuding a quiet confidence that belied the turmoil of emotions churning within her.

"Hey," she called out, her voice firm. "Leave him alone."

The bullies turned, their expressions a mix of surprise and annoyance at the unexpected interruption. But Janet refused to back down, her gaze steady and her stance resolute.

"What's it to you?" One of the older students sneered, his tone laced with a dismissive arrogance.

Janet took a step forward, her eyes narrowing as she spoke. "Because I know what it's like to be in their shoes," she said, her words measured and purposeful. "And I'm not going to stand by and watch you torment someone else."

The bullies exchanged uneasy glances, the weight of Janet's conviction clearly unsettling them. Without another word, they muttered under their breath and slunk away.

Turning her attention to the younger student, Janet offered a warm, reassuring smile. "Are you okay?" she asked, her voice gentle and compassionate.

The victim, his eyes wide with a mixture of fear and gratitude, nodded shakily. "Th-thank you," he managed to stammer out.

Janet reached out and placed a comforting hand on his shoulder. "You don't have to thank me," she said, her expression filled with understanding. "I know how it feels to be on the receiving end of that kind of cruelty. But you don't have to face it alone, okay?"

As Janet walked away, she couldn't help but overhear the whispers of admiration and respect that rippled through the onlookers. That was incredible, one student murmured, their tone laced with awe.

Janet felt a flush of pride spread across her cheeks, but this time, it was not tinged with the self-consciousness that had once defined her. Instead, she recognized the impact of her actions, the way her courage and compassion had inspired those around her. It was a powerful realization, one that reinforced the transformative journey she had undertaken.

And as Janet continued on her way, she knew that this was just the beginning. As the final bell of the day rang, Janet made her way to the familiar doors of the community theater. The confrontations she had faced earlier in the day had only served to strengthen her resolve, igniting a fire within her that refused to be extinguished.

Stepping into the bustling rehearsal area, Janet felt a surge of energy and anticipation wash over her.

As the director called the cast to their places, Janet threw herself into her role with a passion and intensity that surprised even her. Gone were the days of tentative line deliveries and self-conscious movements. In their place stood a young woman who had found the courage to truly inhabit the character, to pour her heart and soul into every word and gesture.

Midway through the rehearsal, the director called for an improvisation exercise, challenging the actors to tap into their own experiences and emotions to breathe life into their performances. Without hesitation, Janet stepped forward, her mind racing as she drew upon the confrontations and triumphs of the day.

What unfolded next was a captivating, raw, and honest monologue that left the entire cast and director spellbound. Janet's words flowed with a palpable intensity, her voice laced with the pain, resilience, and confidence that had become the hallmarks of her transformation.

As she spoke, the theater fell silent, every eye trained on Janet's performance. The director, her own eyes glistening with unshed tears, watched in awe, her expression reflecting the profound impact of Janet's portrayal.

When the monologue came to a close, the cast erupted into thunderous applause, their cheers and accolades washing over her like a tidal wave of validation and support.

In that moment, Janet felt a profound sense of catharsis, a release of the emotions and insecurities that had once held her back. She was now unafraid to be seen, to be heard, and to share the full breadth of her experiences with the world.

The director approached Janet, her expression filled with genuine admiration. "That was truly remarkable," she said, her voice thick with emotion. "The depth of feeling you brought to that scene – it was breathtaking."

Janet felt a flush of pride and disbelief wash over her. There she was, standing tall and confident, her vulnerability now a source of strength rather than weakness.

As the rehearsal continued, Janet was at ease, her movements and delivery imbued with confidence that radiated from every fiber of her being. The theater had become a crucible, forging her into the self-assured young woman she had always had the potential to be. As the rehearsal drew to a close, Janet gathered her belongings, her mind still reeling from the powerful emotional release she had experienced on stage. The theater had become a sanctuary, a place where she could shed the weight of her insecurities and embrace her full potential.

Janet made her way out of the building, her steps light and her spirit buoyed by the support and encouragement of her castmates. But as she turned the corner, a familiar face caught her eye, stopping her in her tracks.

Her oldest brother stood at the entrance of the local convenience store, his gaze briefly meeting Janet's before quickly darting away. For a moment, the sibling simply stared at her, the weight of their tumultuous history palpable in the air.

But then, something shifted. Janet watched as her brother's expression softened, the usual sneer and disdain replaced by a hint of uncertainty and – could it be – remorse?

Hesitantly, he approached her, his movements awkward and his words coming out in a clumsy, halting manner. "Hey, Janet," he began, his voice barely above a whisper. "I, uh, I've noticed some changes in you lately."

Janet felt her heart skip a beat, her initial instinct to retreat warring with a growing curiosity. Cautiously, she held her ground, her gaze steady as she waited for him to continue.

"I just wanted to say..." her brother paused, his brow furrowed in a rare moment of vulnerability. "I'm sorry. For all the times I... you know, I was a jerk to you."

The words hung in the air, their weight undeniable. Janet felt a lump rise in her throat, her eyes stinging with the beginnings of tears. This was a side of her brother she had never seen before – a side stripped of the bravado and cruelty that had once defined their interactions.

"I guess I never really understood how much it hurt you," he continued, his gaze shifting to the ground. "But I see it now, and I'm... I'm sorry."

Janet stood in stunned silence, her mind racing as she processed the unexpected apology. For so long, she had yearned for this moment, for her brothers to acknowledge the pain they had inflicted and to show even a glimmer of remorse. And now, here it was, in this quiet, unassuming moment.

Cautiously, Janet took a step forward, her expression softening. "I... I appreciate that," she said. "It means a lot to me that you're willing to acknowledge it."

Her brother nodded, a flicker of relief crossing his features. "I know it's not enough to just say sorry," he admitted, his gaze meeting hers once more. "But I want you to know that I see you, Janet. I see how much you've changed, and... I'm proud of you."

Janet felt a surge of emotion wash over her, the weight of her brother's words resonating deep within her. This was a turning point, a potential bridge between the fractured relationship they had once shared.

As they parted ways, Janet couldn't help but feel a glimmer of hope take root within her. The journey ahead might not be an easy one, but in this moment, she knew that the first steps towards reconciliation had been taken. And with that realization came a renewed sense of determination – to continue on her path of self-discovery and to forge a stronger, more understanding bond with her family. As Janet made her way home, her mind was still reeling from the unexpected encounter with her brother. The sincere, if clumsy, apology had caught her off guard, opening the door to the possibility of reconciliation and healing within their fractured relationship.

But as she approached the front door, a familiar murmur of voices reached her ears, drawing her attention. Pausing for a moment, Janet realized that her parents were engaged in a hushed conversation in the living room, their tones laced with a mix of pride and concern.

Curiosity piqued, Janet quietly stepped closer, careful not to alert them to her presence. What she overheard next caused her heart to skip a beat.

"I can't believe we didn't see the changes in her sooner," her mother's voice rang out, tinged with a hint of regret. "Our poor girl has been struggling, and we were too blind to notice."

Her father's response was equally weighted with emotion. "I know, dear. We've been so wrapped up in our own lives, we've missed the transformation happening right under our noses. Janet's become a different person, and we need to be there for her."

Janet felt a lump rise in her throat, the realization that her parents had been oblivious to her inner turmoil and the profound changes she had undergone both comforting and disheartening. They cared, she knew, but their own preoccupations had blinded them to the challenges she had faced.

Unable to remain silent any longer, Janet stepped into the living room, her presence immediately drawing the attention of her parents. For a moment, the three of them simply stared at one another, the air thick with a palpable tension.

Then, without a word, Janet crossed the room and enveloped her parents in a tight embrace, the tears she had been holding back finally spilling forth. Her mother and father, caught off guard by the unexpected display of vulnerability, quickly returned the hug, their own eyes glistening with unshed tears.

"I'm sorry," Janet whispered, her voice trembling with emotion. "I'm sorry I didn't feel like I could come to you before. I was just... so afraid."

Her parents held her tighter, their expressions etched with a mixture of guilt and unconditional love. "Oh, sweetheart," her mother murmured, "we're the ones who should be sorry. We should have been there for you, no matter what."

The family remained locked in their embrace, the weight of unspoken words and unresolved tensions slowly dissipating as they allowed themselves to be vulnerable with one another. When they finally pulled apart, Janet could see understanding and determination shining in her parents' eyes.

"We're here for you, Janet," her father said, his voice thick with emotion. "We may not have been the best at showing it before, but we're going to do better. We're going to be the support you need, no matter what."

Janet nodded, her own expression reflecting a cautious hope. "I know," she replied, her words laced with a quiet strength. "And I'm ready to talk. About everything. I want us to be a family again — truly."

As the family settled into a heartfelt discussion, tears were shed and apologies were made. But through it all, a new understanding began to take root, a foundation upon which they could rebuild their fractured relationships and forge a stronger, more supportive bond.

In that moment, Janet knew that she was no longer alone in her journey. Her family, once a source of pain and insecurity, had the potential to become her greatest source of strength and encouragement. And with that realization came a renewed sense of purpose and determination — to continue on her path of self-discovery, with the unconditional support of those who mattered most. As the evening drew to a close, Janet sat at her desk, a well-worn journal open before her. The events of the day had been a whirlwind of emotions, from the confrontations that had once terrified her to the understanding she had forged with her family.

Dipping her pen into the ink, Janet began to write, her words flowing with clarity and purpose. She reflected on the remarkable transformation she had undergone, marveling at the strength and resilience she had discovered within herself.

No longer was she the timid, easily-cowed girl she had once been. Yet, as Janet's pen danced across the page, she acknowledged that the journey was far from over. The scars of her past still lingered, and the insecurities that had once held her back still threatened to resurface, even in the face of her newfound confidence.

But it was in that moment that a spark of inspiration ignited within her. As she contemplated the challenges she had overcome, Janet couldn't help but think of the countless others who were still struggling, still trapped in the shadows of self-doubt and bullying.

With a renewed sense of purpose, she began to formulate a plan – to start a support group at her school, a safe haven where students could find the courage to share their stories and support one another. The idea filled her with a profound sense of excitement and determination, a tangible way to use her voice to empower those who had once been silenced.

Janet's hand moved across the page with urgency, her thoughts racing as she mapped out the details of her vision. She would reach out to the school counselor, gather a team of like-minded individuals, and create a space where those who had once felt alone could find solace and strength in one another.

As she wrote, Janet could feel the weight of her own burdens beginning to lift, replaced by a growing sense of empowerment and purpose. This was her chance to make a difference, to use her experiences to uplift and inspire others who were facing similar struggles.

By the time she finally set down her pen, Janet felt a profound sense of peace and determination wash over her. Tomorrow, she would take the first steps towards realizing her vision, fueled by the knowledge that she was no longer confined to the shadows, but rather, ready to step into the light and share her voice with the world.

With a contented sigh, Janet closed her journal and settled into bed, her mind already buzzing with the possibilities that lay ahead. As she drifted off to sleep, a small, triumphant smile played on her lips, a testament to the remarkable journey she had undertaken and the even greater heights she was poised to reach.

A TRANSFORMATIVE JOURNEY

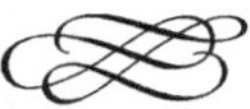

Janet took a deep breath as she pushed open the heavy doors of the community theater, her heart racing with a mix of excitement and trepidation. The energy that greeted her was both exhilarating and daunting, a stark contrast to the quiet solitude she had grown accustomed to.

As Janet entered the enclosed space, her gaze was immediately caught by the seasoned performers that were effortlessly rehearsing their lines and performing flawlessly complex stage movements. She watched in awe, feeling a familiar pang of self-doubt as she compared her own tentative skills to their polished expertise.

"You must be Janet," a warm voice called out, snapping her from her reverie. A tall, elegant woman approached, her presence commanding the attention of the room. "I'm Evelyn, the workshop leader. Welcome to our intensive weekend."

Janet offered a tentative smile, her fingers fidgeting nervously. "It's nice to meet you," she replied.

Evelyn's expression softened as she placed a reassuring hand on Janet's shoulder. "I know it can be intimidating, being surrounded by so much talent," she said, her tone gentle. "But I can see the potential in you, and I'm excited to help you unlock it."

Gathering the group, Evelyn's voice rang out, commanding the attention of the noisy room. "Over the next two days, we're going to be exploring the very heart of what it means to be an actor," she began, her gaze sweeping across the faces of the aspiring performers. "That means digging deep, tapping into our vulnerabilities, and taking risks like we've never taken before."

Janet felt a shiver of apprehension run down her spine, but beneath the surface, a spark of determination began to ignite. She had come here to push her boundaries, to shed the timid shell that had confined her for so long. And as Evelyn outlined the challenging exercises that lay ahead, Janet steeled her resolve, determined to embrace the vulnerability and risk-taking that were the hallmarks of true artistry.

"Acting is not just about memorizing lines and hitting your marks," Evelyn continued, her gaze settling on Janet for a moment. "It's about baring your soul, exposing the rawest parts of yourself, and using that to breathe life into the characters you portray."

Janet nodded, her mind racing as she contemplated the daunting task before her. But as she looked around at the eager faces of her fellow workshop participants, she felt a glimmer of hope take root. These were individuals who understood the power of self-expression, who were willing to confront their own fears and insecurities in pursuit of their artistic passions.

And in that moment, Janet knew that she was no longer alone in her journey. With a sense of determination, she steeled herself for the challenges that lay ahead, ready to shed the last vestiges of her self-doubt and embrace the transformative power of the stage.

Janet's palms grew clammy as Evelyn divided the group into pairs, her heart pounding with a familiar sense of uneasiness. When the woman called out her name, paired with a confident-looking young man named Marcus, Janet felt her stomach twist into knots.

"Alright, everyone," Evelyn's voice rang out, "for this next exercise, you and your partner will need to trust each other completely. One person will fall backward, and the other will catch them. Then, you'll switch roles."

Janet turned to Marcus, her expression a mixture of apprehension and uncertainty. "I-I don't know if I can do this," she stammered, her gaze darting around the room.

Marcus offered her a warm, reassuring smile. "Hey, no need to be nervous," he said, his tone gentle. "I know it can be scary at first, but I've got you. We'll take it slow, okay?"

Reluctantly, Janet nodded, her fingers fidgeting with the hem of her shirt. She watched as Marcus positioned himself, his body poised and ready to catch her. With a deep breath, she forced herself to turn around, her eyes squeezed shut as she prepared to fall.

"I'm right here," Marcus murmured, his voice a calming anchor in the storm of Janet's nerves. "Whenever you're ready."

Summoning every ounce of courage she could muster, Janet leaned back, her body surrendering to the trust she was placing in her partner. For a heartbeat, she felt the world tilt, the familiar sensation of falling sending a jolt of panic through her. But then, strong arms enveloped her, steadying her as she was gently lowered to the ground.

Janet's eyes flew open, a gasp of surprise escaping her lips. The exhilaration of being caught, of having her trust rewarded, sent a surge of adrenaline coursing through her veins. She met Marcus's gaze, with respect and admiration shining in her eyes.

"See?" he said, his smile widening. "I told you I've got you."

As they switched roles, Janet felt a shift within her. Gone was the hesitation and self-doubt; in its place, a growing sense of responsibility and strength blossomed. Carefully, she reached out, her arms steadying Marcus as he fell back into her embrace.

The weight of his trust, the knowledge that she held his well-being in her hands, filled Janet with a profound sense of purpose. She had been the one to be caught, to be supported, and now, it was her turn to be the pillar of strength.

As the exercise continued, Janet grew more and more comfortable with the vulnerability that was required.

The initial concern slowly gave way to a sense of empowerment, a realization that she could not only trust others but also be trusted in return.

When the exercise finally came to an end, Evelyn's voice rang out, her expression filled with pride. "Excellent work, everyone," she said, her gaze settling on Janet for a moment. "I can see the trust and connection you've built with your partners. That's the foundation of great acting – being able to truly see and support one another."

Janet felt a flush of pride spread across her cheeks, the weight of Evelyn's words resonating deep within her. This was just the beginning, she knew, of a transformative journey that would push her far beyond the boundaries she had once accepted as her own. As the morning session drew to a close, Evelyn gathered the group for the next exercise, her expression shifting to one of profound seriousness.

Now, she began, her voice carrying a weight that commanded the attention of the room, this next exercise is all about tapping into your deepest emotions. I want you to draw upon your own personal experiences, your joys and your pains, and use that to fuel your performances.

Janet felt a familiar knot of apprehension form in the pit of her stomach. Personal experiences? she thought, her mind racing. How could she possibly expose the raw, vulnerable parts of herself in front of this group of strangers?

But as Evelyn began to call out names, pairing the participants for a series of intense confrontation scenes, Janet found her resolve hardening. She watched, transfixed, as her fellow actors poured their hearts into their performances, their faces etched with raw emotion.

When Evelyn finally called her name, paired with a seasoned actress, Janet felt an increased concern. But as she stepped forward, a familiar memory began to surface – the taunts and jeers of her brothers, the cruel laughter that had once defined her childhood.

With a deep breath, Janet allowed the emotions to wash over her, the pain and resentment she had long suppressed bubbling to the surface. As the scene unfolded, her voice rang out, laced with a palpable intensity that seemed to reverberate through the theater.

She channeled every ounce of her personal experience, the years of torment and self-doubt, into her performance, her body language and facial expressions conveying the raw vulnerability of her character. The other actors watched, transfixed, as Janet's portrayal unfolded before them, several observers wiping away tears as they were moved by the sheer authenticity of her work.

When the scene finally came to a close, the theater fell silent, the weight of Janet's performance palpable in the air. Then, Evelyn's voice broke the spell, her expression filled with a profound sense of awe.

"That," she said, her tone thick with emotion, "was truly remarkable. The depth of feeling you brought to that moment – it was breathtaking."

Janet felt a flush of pride and disbelief wash over her. She had always been the shy, insecure girl, the one who shrank away from the spotlight. But here she was, standing tall and confident, her vulnerability now a source of strength rather than weakness.

Evelyn's gaze settled on her, a warm smile spreading across her face. "Janet," she said, "your bravery in tapping into your own experiences is truly inspiring. You've shown us all that personal pain can be transformed into compelling art."

As the workshop continued, Janet found herself more at ease, her performances imbued with a confidence that radiated from every fiber of her being. The theater had become a crucible, forging her into the self-assured young woman she had always had the potential to be. As the morning session came to a close, Janet was drawn to a group of actors gathered in the theater's small cafeteria. They were engaged in an animated discussion, their voices filled with a palpable passion that piqued Janet's curiosity.

Hesitantly, she approached the group, her fingers fidgeting with the hem of her shirt. "Excuse me," she began, her voice barely above a whisper, "do you mind if I join you?"

The actors turned, their expressions immediately shifting to ones of warmth and welcome. "Of course!" One of them exclaimed, gesturing to an empty seat. "Pull up a chair."

Janet felt a flush of relief as she settled into the spot, her gaze shifting from one face to the next as the group resumed their conversation. They were discussing their creative processes, each actor offering insights and techniques that had helped them in their pursuit of the craft.

Janet listened intently, her mind racing as she absorbed every word. She had always been the silent observer, content to watch from the sidelines, but something about the energy and camaraderie of this group drew her in.

When one of the actors turned to her, a curious expression on his face, Janet felt a familiar wave of self-consciousness wash over her. "How about you?" he asked, his tone genuinely interested. "What's your approach to building a character?"

For a moment, Janet hesitated, her gaze shifting to the floor. But then, a memory surfaced – the taunts and jeers of her brothers, the cruel laughter that had once defined her childhood. With a deep breath, she met the actor's gaze, her voice steadier than she had expected.

"Well," she began, her words measured and purposeful, "I've found that drawing on my own personal experiences can be really powerful. Especially when it comes to portraying characters who've faced adversity or bullying."

The group fell silent, their expressions shifting to ones of rapt attention. "Go on," one of the actors encouraged, his eyes shining with genuine interest.

Janet felt a surge of courage course through her veins. "Well, you see," she continued, "I've had my own struggles with bullying, particularly from my brothers. And I've found that channeling that pain and resentment into my performances can make them feel so much more authentic and raw."

The actors nodded, their faces etched with understanding and empathy. One by one, they began to share their own stories – tales of overcoming personal challenges through the power of story-telling and self-expression.

Janet listened, her heart swelling with a sense of kinship and belonging. These were individuals who understood the transformative power of art, who had found solace and strength in the act of creating. She knew that she had found her people.

As the conversation continued, she felt the last vestiges of her self-consciousness melt away. She shared more of her experiences, her voice growing stronger and more confident with each passing minute. And with every nod of understanding, every word of encouragement, she felt a deep sense of validation – a realization that her struggles were not hers alone, but part of a shared journey that bound this community of storytellers together.

When the lunch break drew to a close, Janet felt reluctant to part ways with her newfound companions. But as she rose to her feet, she knew that she had discovered something far more valuable than a simple meal – she had found a place where she truly belonged. As the afternoon session began, Janet felt a familiar flutter of nerves in the pit of her stomach. While the emotional recall exercise in the morning was intense and elevated her to new levels, the idea of venturing into physical theater made her anxious.

Janet had always been self-conscious about her body, the lingering effects of her brothers' taunts and the cruel judgments of her peers making it difficult for her to fully embrace her physical self. But as Evelyn gathered the group and outlined the upcoming exercises, Janet decided to confront her insecurities head-on.

The first exercise involved using the entire body to convey emotion and tell stories without the aid of words. Janet watched, transfixed, as her fellow actors moved with a grace and expressiveness that seemed to defy gravity. Their limbs twisted and contorted, their faces etched with a range of emotions that captivated the onlookers.

When Evelyn called on her to step forward, Janet felt a familiar wave of panic wash over her. But as she took her place in the center of the room, she forced herself to take a deep breath and let go of her inhibitions.

Slowly, she began to move, her body responding to the emotional cues Evelyn provided. At first, she was hesitant, her eyes darting around as she tried to calm down. But as the exercise continued, something inside her changed.

Janet felt freedom in the way her body moved, a sense of liberation that she had never experienced before. She allowed her limbs to flow and bend, her face mirroring the emotions she was portraying – joy, sorrow, determination, and everything in between.

By the time the exercise drew to a close, Janet was breathless, but her eyes were shining with a sense of accomplishment. She had stepped out of her comfort zone, confronting her deepest insecurities, and in doing so, she had discovered a profound appreciation for the expressive power of her physical self.

Evelyn's voice rang out, her expression filled with pride. "Janet," she said, "your willingness to take risks and fully immerse yourself in that exercise was truly inspiring. The way you used your body to convey such a range of emotions – it was remarkable."

Janet felt a flush of pride spread across her cheeks, the weight of Evelyn's words resonating deep within her. For so long, she had viewed her body as a source of shame and insecurity, but in this moment, she realized that it was a powerful tool, a means of self-expression and storytelling that she had only begun to unlock.

As the afternoon session continued, Janet felt more and more at ease, her movements becoming increasingly fluid and expressive.

She reveled in the freedom of letting her body speak, of using every inch of her physical form to bring the characters she portrayed to life.

And with each passing exercise, she could feel, for the first time, appreciation for her body blossoming within her. No longer was it a source of self-consciousness and doubt, but rather, a vessel for her creativity and self-expression – a confirmation of the transformative power of stepping out of one's comfort zone and embracing the full breadth of one's potential. As the afternoon session progressed, Evelyn gathered the group for a scene study exercise, pairing the participants in intense confrontation scenes. Janet felt the familiar flutter of nerves as the woman called her name, coupling her with a seasoned actress whose presence commanded the attention of the room.

Alright, Evelyn announced, her voice ringing out with authority, I want you all to dig deep and tap into the raw emotions you explored this morning. This is about more than just reciting lines – it's about truly embodying your characters and letting the conflict between them come alive.

Janet turned to her scene partner, a woman named Sophia, whose piercing gaze immediately set her on edge. As they began to rehearse the confrontational dialogue, Janet struggled watching Sophia's intensity. Her words felt hollow, her movements stilted, and she could see the frustration building in her partner's expression.

Sensing the tension, Evelyn approached the pair, her brow furrowed in concentration. "Janet," she said, her tone gentle yet firm, "I can see you're holding back. What is it that's keeping you from fully embracing this moment?"

Janet felt her cheeks flush with embarrassment, the weight of Evelyn's gaze making her squirm. I-I don't know," she stammered, her gaze shifting to the floor. "I just can't seem to... to find the right intensity."

Evelyn nodded, her expression thoughtful. "Janet," she said, "I want you to think back to the emotional recall exercise this morning. Remember the raw emotion you tapped into, the pain and resentment you channeled into your performance. That's the key here."

Janet's mind raced as she recalled the experience, the way she had allowed the memories of her brothers' taunts to fuel her portrayal of the confrontational character. Closing her eyes, she took a deep breath, allowing those emotions to wash over her once more.

When she opened them, determination had settled in her gaze. Turning to Sophia, she launched into the scene, her voice laced with a palpable intensity that seemed to reverberate through the theater. Her movements were no longer stilted, but rather, fluid and expressive, every gesture and facial expression imbued with the weight of her personal experiences.

Sophia's eyes widened, her own performance rising to match Janet's intensity. The two women engaged in a captivating dance of confrontation, their characters' conflict mirroring the raw power of their exchange.

By the time the scene drew to a close, the theater was silent, the audience members visibly moved by the raw authenticity of the performance. Evelyn approached the pair, her expression filled with a profound sense of awe.

"Janet," she said, her voice thick with emotion, "that was truly remarkable. The way you tapped into your own experiences to fuel your portrayal – it was breathtaking."

Janet felt a surge of pride and disbelief wash over her. She had never imagined herself capable of such a powerful, emotionally-charged performance. And as she met Sophia's gaze, she saw a newfound respect and understanding reflected in the other woman's eyes.

In that moment, Janet knew that she had taken a monumental step forward in her journey of self-discovery. The walls she had built up over the years crumbled, and in their place stood a young woman who was unafraid to confront her deepest fears and insecurities, using them as the fuel to ignite her artistic passions. As the afternoon session drew to a close, Evelyn gathered the group for a final reflection exercise, her expression filled with a profound sense of pride.

"Today has been a whirlwind," she began, her gaze sweeping across the faces of the aspiring performers. "You've all pushed yourselves to new heights, confronting your fears and vulnerabilities in ways that have truly transformed your work."

Janet felt a familiar flutter of nerves as Evelyn's eyes settled on her for a moment, but this time, the sensation was tempered by a growing sense of confidence and self-assurance.

Now, the workshop leader continued, "I want each of you to share your biggest challenge and triumph of the day. What did you learn about yourself, and how will you take that forward?"

One by one, the participants shared their experiences, their voices laced with a mix of vulnerability and pride. Some spoke of overcoming stage fright, others of tapping into the depths of their emotional reservoir. But as Janet listened, she couldn't help but feel a growing sense of kinship with these individuals, each of them on their own journey of self-discovery.

When Evelyn finally called her name, Janet felt a surge of trepidation, but this time, it was tempered by determination. Taking a deep breath, she rose to her feet, her gaze sweeping across the faces of her fellow workshop participants.

"My biggest challenge," she began, her voice steady and clear, "has been overcoming my fear of being seen and judged. For so long, I've hidden behind a veil of insecurity, afraid to let my true self shine through."

The group fell silent, their expressions reflecting a profound sense of empathy and understanding. But as Janet continued, her words gaining momentum, a palpable shift could be felt in the room.

"But today," she said, her voice growing stronger with each passing moment, "I've learned that vulnerability is not a weakness, but a strength. By tapping into my own experiences, my own pain and triumphs, I've discovered a well of creativity and self-expression that I never knew existed."

Janet paused, her gaze sweeping across the faces of her captivated audience. "And for that," she continued, her tone laced with a profound sense of gratitude, "I want to thank all of you. This supportive environment, this community of storytellers – you've helped me find my voice, and I'm forever grateful".

As Janet's words faded, the theater erupted into thunderous applause, the other participants rising to their feet in a display of heartfelt admiration. Several of them approached Janet afterwards, their expressions filled with a mix of awe and inspiration.

"Your journey is so incredible," one of the actors exclaimed, her eyes shining with unshed tears. "You've inspired all of us to be braver, to confront our own fears and insecurities."

Janet felt a flush of pride and humility wash over her. She had never imagined that her story, her struggles, could have such a profound impact on those around her. But in that moment, she realized that by embracing her vulnerability, she had tapped into a wellspring of strength and resilience that resonated with her fellow performers.

As the group dispersed, Janet lingered in the theater, her mind racing with the events of the day. She had come to this workshop with a heart full of anxiety, but now, she felt a renewed sense of purpose and determination – a conviction that she was on the cusp of something truly transformative.

With a contented smile, she gathered her belongings and made her way out into the cool evening air, her steps lighter and her spirit buoyed by the knowledge that she was no longer alone in her journey of self-discovery. As the evening shadows began to lengthen, Janet stepped out of the community theater, her body physically exhausted but her mind and spirit soaring with energy and purpose.

The day had been a whirlwind of emotions, challenges, and personal triumphs, and as Janet made her way through the quiet streets, she couldn't help but reflect on just how much she had grown since first stepping onto that stage.

Gone was the timid, self-conscious girl who had once shrunk from the spotlight, her insecurities and fears holding her back. In her place stood a young woman who had confronted her deepest vulnerabilities, using them as the fuel to ignite her artistic passions.

Janet felt a surge of pride swell within her, a profound sense of accomplishment that she had never experienced before. The walls she had built up over the years were slowly crumbling, and in their place stood confidence and self-assurance that radiated from every fiber of her being.

As she walked, Janet couldn't help but marvel at the transformation she had undergone. The rigorous exercises and emotional outpouring, combined with the encouragement from her fellow performers – it had all coalesced into a transformative experience that had left a permanent mark on her soul.

No longer did she view the stage as a source of fear and trepidation, but rather, as a sanctuary where she could fully embrace her creativity and self-expression. The theater had become a crucible, forging her into the confident, empowered young woman she had always had the potential to be.

And as Janet's steps carried her closer to home, she felt a rush of excitement and determination running through her. She knew that this was just the beginning of a journey that would continue to push her boundaries and challenge her preconceptions.

With a silent promise to herself, Janet vowed to bring this confidence and expressiveness into every aspect of her life, both on and off the stage. No longer would she allow her insecurities to hold her back, but rather, she would embrace the power of her voice, her body, and her unique perspective, using them to inspire and uplift those around her.

The weight of her transformation was palpable, a tangible shift in her demeanor and bearing that was impossible to ignore. Janet walked with a new sense of purpose, her head held high and her steps filled with a quiet determination that belied the turmoil of emotions she had faced throughout the day.

As she reached her front door, she paused, taking a moment to savor the profound sense of accomplishment and belonging that had blossomed within her. She knew that this was a turning point, a pivotal moment in her journey of self-discovery that would continue to shape and define the person she would become.

With a contented sigh, Janet pushed open the door, her mind already racing with the possibilities that lay ahead. The future was hers to shape, and she was more than ready to embrace it.

INSPIRING OTHERS

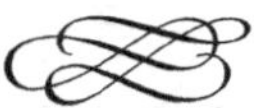

Janet was nervous. This was the moment she had been both anticipating and dreading – the opportunity to share her personal journey of self-discovery through the power of theater.

Taking a deep breath, she glanced around the room, her gaze briefly meeting the encouraging smile of her teacher. Liam's words of support echoed in her mind, reminding her of the strength she had found on stage. With a steadying exhale, she began to speak, her voice trembling slightly at first.

"Over the past few months, I've been on a remarkable journey of self-discovery," Janet began, her words measured and purposeful. "It all started when I stepped out of my comfort zone and into the world of theater."

The class fell silent, their attention fixed on Janet as she shared her personal anecdotes. She spoke of the insecurities that had once held her back, the taunts and jeers of her brothers that had chipped away at her self-worth. But then, she recounted the transformative experience of her first performance, the way the stage had become a sanctuary where she could fully embrace her authentic self.

As Janet's voice grew stronger, her classmates began to nod in recognition, their expressions reflecting the weight of their own struggles. She described the support she had found within the theater community, the way her newfound confidence had empowered her to stand up to her siblings' cruelty.

Janet's teacher, Ms. Winters, watched the proceedings with a growing sense of pride, her eyes shining with unshed tears. She had witnessed the remarkable transformation in her once-shy student, and in this moment, she saw the full blossoming of Janet's courage and self-assurance.

"It hasn't been an easy journey," Janet continued, her gaze sweeping across the faces of her captivated audience. "But through the power of storytelling and self-expression, I've discovered a strength within myself that I never knew existed."

The classroom erupted in a smattering of applause, several of Janet's peers offering nods of understanding and admiration. In that moment, Janet felt a surge of pride and accomplishment wash over her, the weight of her own words resonating deep within her soul.

She had come so far, from the timid, insecure girl who had once shrunk from the spotlight to the young woman who now stood tall, her voice clear and firm. And as she met the gaze of her class-mates, she knew that her journey had only just begun — a confir-mation to the transformative power of finding one's voice and the courage to share it with the world. As the lunch bell rang, Janet scanned the busy cafeteria, her gaze settling on a familiar sight — a younger student, hunched over and trying to make herself as small as possible, clearly attempting to avoid attention.

The image struck a chord within Janet, a poignant reminder of her own past struggles with insecurity and self-consciousness. Without hesitation, she made her way across the room, a warm smile spreading across her face as she approached the girl.

"Hi, I'm Janet," she said, her voice gentle and welcoming. "I couldn't help but notice you sitting over here all by yourself. Would you like to join me and my friends?"

The girl's eyes widened, a mix of surprise and uncertainty flashing across her features. Janet could see the walls of self-protection slowly beginning to crumble as she extended the invitation.

"I-I don't know," the girl stammered, her gaze shifting nervously. "I don't want to intrude."

"Not at all," Janet reassured her, her expression radiating kindness. "We'd love to have you. Come on, let me introduce you."

Gently, she placed a hand on the girl's shoulder, guiding her towards the table where Janet's friends were gathered. As they approached, Janet shared a bit about her own journey with confidence.

"You know, I used to be a lot like you," she said, her tone laced with empathy. "I used to avoid attention and try to blend into the background. But then I discovered the power of theater, and it changed everything."

The girl's posture visibly relaxed, a small smile forming on her lips as she listened to Janet's story. The warmth and acceptance that emanated from the group was palpable, and Janet could see the tension slowly seeping from the girl's shoulders.

"Welcome to the group," one of Janet's friends chimed in, offering the newcomer a friendly smile. "We're always happy to have new faces around here."

As the girl settled in, Janet felt a surge of pride and accomplishment wash over her. She had once been in the girl's shoes, desperately seeking a sense of belonging and acceptance. And now, she had the opportunity to extend that same kindness and support to someone who needed it.

In that moment, she realized that her journey of self-discovery had come full circle. By reaching out and offering a helping hand, she was not only uplifting the girl before her but also continuing to heal and empower herself. It was a confirmation of the transformative power of empathy and the profound impact that one person could have on another.

As Janet made her way to her drama class, the familiar flutter of nerves stirred in the pit of her stomach. The teacher had announced a special project – an opportunity for students to create and perform monologues about a personal challenge they had overcome.

Janet felt a mix of excitement and anxiety as she settled into her seat, her mind racing with the possibilities. Just a few months ago, the thought of standing up in front of her peers and sharing such a personal story would have been unthinkable. But now, after her transformative journey, she was brimming with experiences to draw from.

Closing her eyes, Janet allowed her mind to wander back to the night of her first performance, the memory of that pivotal moment still etching itself into her soul. The trembling hands, the pounding heart, the overwhelming sense of fear – it had all melted away the moment she had stepped onto that stage, her voice finding a strength and conviction she had never known.

With a determined nod, she began to jot down her ideas, her pen moving across the page with fluency. She would write about that night, the way it had sparked a profound change within her, and how the support of the theater community had helped her to over-come her deepest insecurities.

As Janet worked, she couldn't help but notice the growing frustra-tion on the faces of her classmates. Many of them seemed to be struggling with the assignment, their brows furrowed in concen-tration as they stared at blank pages.

Hesitantly, Janet approached one of her peers, a shy girl named Emma, who was chewing nervously on the end of her pen.

"Hey, are you having trouble with the project?" Janet asked, her voice laced with empathy.

Emma's gaze snapped up, a flush of embarrassment spreading across her cheeks. "I-I just don't know what to write about," she admitted, her shoulders slumping in defeat.

Janet offered her a reassuring smile, a spark of confidence igniting within her. "Well, why don't you tell me a bit about what you've been through?" she suggested, her tone gentle and encouraging. "I'd be happy to help you brainstorm some ideas."

To Janet's surprise, the words flowed with ease, her own experi-ences providing a wellspring of insight and understanding. As she listened to Emma's story and offered suggestions, she realized just how much she had grown – from the timid, self-conscious girl who had once avoided confrontation to the young woman who now felt empowered to support and uplift her peers.

By the time the class drew to a close, Janet had assisted several of her classmates, each one leaving with a new sense of direction and enthusiasm for the project. As she gathered her belongings, she couldn't help but feel a swell of pride – not only in her own progress but in the realization that she now had the confidence and compassion to help others find their own voice. The final bell had barely rung when Janet went to the guidance counselor's office, her heart pounding with a mix of nerves and determination.

After her transformative experiences in the theater community, Janet had been struck by a profound realization – the power of finding one's voice and the profound impact it could have on those struggling with issues like bullying and low self-esteem. And now, she was determined to share that revelation with others, to create a safe space where students could come together and support one another.

Taking a deep breath, she pushed open the door, her gaze settling on the kind, bespectacled face of Mrs. Simmons, the school's guidance counselor.

"Janet, what a pleasant surprise," the woman greeted her, a warm smile spreading across her features. "How can I help you today?"

Janet felt a surge of courage course through her veins as she launched into her proposal, her words flowing with confidence and conviction.

"Mrs. Simmons, I've been thinking a lot about the challenges that so many students face – the bullying, the insecurities, the struggle to find their voice," she began, firmly. "And I believe that I may have a way to help."

The counselor leaned forward, her expression one of rapt attention as Janet outlined her vision for a student-led support group. She spoke passionately about her own journey, the way the theater community had become a sanctuary where she could embrace her authentic self, and how she wanted to extend that same sense of belonging and empowerment to others.

As Janet's presentation drew to a close, Mrs. Simmons sat back in her chair, her eyes shining with a mix of pride and admiration.

"Janet, this is an incredible idea," she said, her voice thick with emotion. "The insights you've gained, the personal experiences you can draw from – it's exactly the kind of support our students need."

Together, they began to outline the framework for the group, with Janet taking on a leadership role. The counselor listened intently, offering suggestions and guidance as they mapped out the logistics and potential activities.

By the time Janet left the office, her steps were lighter, a profound sense of purpose and excitement coursing through her veins. She had taken a leap, stepping out of her comfort zone to share her vision, and in doing so, she had tapped into a wellspring of strength and conviction that she never knew existed.

As she made her way home, Janet couldn't help but reflect on how far she had come. From the timid, insecure girl who had once shrunk from the spotlight to the young woman who now stood ready to uplift and empower her peers – it was a transformation that filled her heart with a deep sense of pride and accomplishment.

And in that moment, she knew that this was just the beginning. With the support of the guidance counselor and the theater community behind her, she was poised to make a real difference in the lives of those who, like her, had once struggled to find their voice.

As Janet made her way through the home's front door, the familiar sounds of her brothers' voices drifted down the hallway, piquing her curiosity. Pausing for a moment, she strained to listen, her brow furrowing in confusion as she realized they were not engaged in their usual taunts and jeers.

Cautiously, Janet crept closer, her heart pounding in her chest as she caught snippets of their conversation. To her surprise, her brothers were speaking in hushed tones, their voices laced with a mix of admiration and uncertainty.

"I can't believe how much she's changed," the youngest one murmured, a hint of guilt evident in his tone. "I feel awful about how we used to treat her."

Janet's eyes widened, the weight of his words settling heavily in the pit of her stomach. For years, she had endured their cruel laughter and relentless ridicule, the scars of their bullying still etching themselves into her psyche. But now, it seemed that something had shifted.

Pausing for a moment, she considered her next move. Should she simply retreat to her room, allowing the conversation to fade into the background?

With a deep, steadying breath, Janet stepped forward, the floorboards creaking beneath her feet and drawing the attention of her siblings. They spun around, their expressions a mix of surprise and unease as they registered her presence.

"Janet," the eldest brother stammered, his gaze shifting nervously. "We, uh, we didn't hear you come in."

Mustering every ounce of courage she possessed, Janet met their gazes, her voice calm and measured. "I couldn't help but overhear what you were talking about," she began, her words carefully chosen. "And I think... I think we need to have an open conversation about our relationship. About how we can move forward from here."

The brothers exchanged uncertain glances, the tension palpable in the air. But to Janet's surprise, they both nodded, their expressions softening with a glimmer of understanding.

"You're right," the youngest brother replied, his tone laced with remorse. "We... we need to talk about this. About how we've treated you, and how we can make things right."

Slowly, the three siblings settled into the living room, the air thick with a mix of vulnerability and apprehension. Janet could feel her heart racing, the weight of years of pain and resentment threatening to spill over. But as the conversation unfolded, the remarkable transformation was noticeable.

Her brothers, once so quick to ridicule and taunt, now spoke with a newfound humility and empathy, acknowledging the harm they had caused and expressing a genuine desire to make amends. And as Janet listened, her own walls of self-protection crumbled, allowing her to share the depth of her hurt and the longing she had always felt for their acceptance.

It was an awkward, halting dialogue, laced with moments of uncomfortable silence and uncertain glances. But beneath the surface, a profound shift was taking place – through open communication and a willingness to understand one another, the fractured bonds of their family began to heal.

As the conversation drew to a close, Janet felt a weight lift from her shoulders, a sense of cautious optimism taking root in her heart. The road ahead would not be an easy one, she knew, but in this moment, she recognized the power of vulnerability, of confronting the past in order to forge a brighter future.

The next day, Janet made her way to the theater. The familiar energy of the community theater buzzed around her as she stepped through the heavy double doors, her heart swelling with excitement. Over the past few months, this space had become a sanctuary, a place where she could fully embrace her passion for the stage and the art of storytelling.

As Janet made her way towards the rehearsal space, Evelyn, the director, approached her with a warm smile.

"Janet," she said, her tone laced with a hint of excitement, "I have a special opportunity for you today."

Janet felt a flutter of nerves in the pit of her stomach, her mind racing with a dozen possibilities. "What is it?" she asked.

Evelyn placed a gentle hand on Janet's shoulder, her expression radiating encouragement. "I'd like you to direct one of the scenes in our upcoming production," she revealed, her eyes shining with a profound sense of trust. "I've been so impressed with the growth and leadership you've shown in our workshops, and I think this is the perfect chance for you to put those skills into practice."

For a moment, Janet felt as if the air had been knocked from her lungs. Direct a scene? The very thought sent a wave of apprehension coursing through her veins. Just a few months ago, the idea of standing before her peers, let alone guiding them through the creative process, would have been utterly unthinkable.

But as Evelyn's words sank in, Janet felt a spark of determination ignite within her. She had come so far, confronting her deepest insecurities and embracing the transformative power of the stage. And now, she had the opportunity to put that growth and confidence to the test.

Squaring her shoulders, she nodded, a resolute expression settling on her features. "I'd be honored," she replied, her voice steadier than she had expected.

As the rehearsal commenced, she was drawing upon the techniques and insights she had gained over the past months. Tentatively at first, she offered suggestions to her fellow actors, guiding them through the emotional beats of the scene and encouraging them to explore new layers of their characters.

To her surprise, the words flowed with a newfound fluency, her confidence growing with each passing moment. She recognized the subtle nuances of body language, the power of pauses and inflection, and the importance of fostering a collaborative, supportive environment.

Evelyn observed from the sidelines, her expression, one of quiet pride as she watched Janet's natural leadership and creativity unfold. The cast, too, responded with enthusiasm, their performances growing richer and more dynamic under Janet's guidance.

When the scene finally came to a close, the theater erupted in thunderous applause, the actors surrounding Janet with expressions of gratitude and admiration.

"That was incredible, Janet," one of them exclaimed, her eyes shining with excitement. "Your direction really helped me unlock a whole new dimension to my character."

Janet felt a flush of pride and disbelief wash over her. Just a few short months ago, she had been the timid, insecure girl, shrinking from the spotlight and the prospect of creative leadership. But now, she stood tall, her confidence radiating from every fiber of her being.

As Evelyn approached, a warm smile spreading across her face, Janet knew that this moment marked yet another milestone in her transformative journey. The road ahead may have been paved with challenges, but in this instant, she recognized the power of her own growth, the remarkable strides she had taken in embracing her unique voice and talents. As she made her way through the bustling hallways, her mind still reeling from the exhilaration of her directorial debut, a familiar voice called out to her.

"Janet! Hey, wait up!"

Turning, she found Liam hurrying towards her, his expression alight with excitement. Janet felt a flutter of anticipation in her chest, her friendship with the kind-hearted young man having blossomed into a source of unconditional support and encouragement over the past few months.

"Liam, hi," she greeted him, a warm smile spreading across her face. "What's going on?"

"You're not going to believe this," Liam began, his words tumbling out in a rush, "but there's a regional theater competition coming up, and I think you should enter!"

Janet felt a familiar wave of trepidation wash over her, her mind immediately conjuring up images of standing on a stage, all eyes fixed upon her. The thought sent a jolt of anxiety through her veins, and for a moment, she found herself at a loss for words.

Sensing her hesitation, Liam placed a reassuring hand on her shoulder, his expression radiating confidence. "Janet, you've come so far," he said, his voice laced with conviction. "The work you've been doing in the theater – it's been incredible to witness. And I know you have what it takes to compete at this level."

Janet chewed on her lower lip, her gaze shifting nervously. "But what if I mess up?" she murmured, the familiar specter of self-doubt rearing its head. "What if I'm not good enough?"

Liam shook his head emphatically. "That's not going to happen," he insisted. "You've grown so much, both as a performer and as a person. This is your chance to show the world what you're capable of."

As Liam outlined the details of the competition, she felt a spark of excitement beginning to ignite within her. The opportunity to showcase her talents on a regional stage, to potentially inspire others with her journey – it was a prospect that both thrilled and terrified her.

Closing her eyes, Janet allowed her mind to wander back to those early days, when the mere thought of stepping onto a stage had filled her with crippling anxiety. She remembered the taunts of her brothers, the cruel laughter that had once defined her existence. But then, she recalled the transformative power of that first performance, the way the theater had changed her life. It was a sanctuary where she could fully embrace her authentic self.

And in that moment, Janet knew that she could not let this chance slip through her fingers. This was more than just a competition – it was a chance to push her boundaries, to inspire others, and to continue the remarkable journey of self-discovery she had embarked upon.

With a deep, steadying breath, Janet met Liam's gaze, with determination etched on her features. "Okay," she said, her voice firm. "I'll do it."

Liam's face lit up with a triumphant grin, and he pulled Janet into a warm embrace. "I knew you could do it," he murmured, his tone laced with pride. "This is going to be amazing, I just know it."

As they began to discuss potential monologues and the preparation involved, Janet felt a mix of nerves and excitement through her veins. But this time, the fear was tempered by a growing sense of confidence, a recognition that she was no longer the same timid, insecure girl who had once shied away from the spotlight.

She was a young woman transformed, empowered by the support of her friends, the lessons she had learned on the stage, and the profound realization that her voice, her story, had the power to touch and inspire others. And with that knowledge firmly rooted in her heart, Janet knew that she was ready to take on this new challenge, embracing it as yet another step in her remarkable journey of self-discovery.

As she stepped into the small, cozy room, her gaze swept across the faces of the diverse group of students gathered there. Some were fidgeting nervously, their expressions a mix of uncertainty and apprehension, while others sat with their arms folded, their posture guarded and defensive.

This was it – the first meeting of the support group Janet had worked tirelessly to establish, a safe space where young people could come together to share their struggles and find the courage to overcome them. And as she stood before the group, Janet couldn't help but feel a profound sense of purpose and responsibility.

Taking a deep breath, she stepped forward, her confident posture and warm smile immediately drawing the attention of the room. For a moment, the students fell silent, their eyes fixed upon her, and Janet felt a familiar flutter of nerves in the pit of her stomach.

But then, she remembered the journey that had brought her to this moment. And with that, she began to speak, her voice clear and firm.

"Hi, everyone," she began, her gaze sweeping across the faces before her. "My name is Janet, and I'm so glad you're all here today."

A hush fell over the room as the students listened, their expressions shifting from apprehension to a glimmer of recognition. Janet could see it in their eyes – the shared experiences, the echoes of her own struggles, and the hope that this gathering might offer a path towards healing and empowerment.

"I know what it's like to feel alone, to be the target of bullying and ridicule," Janet continued, her words laced with empathy. "For a long time, I felt like I didn't have a voice, that I had to shrink away from the world to avoid being hurt."

Several of the students nodded, their posture relaxing as they felt the weight of her words resonate within them.

"But then, I discovered the power of finding my voice – through theater, through self-expression, and through the support of an amazing community. And I realized that my story, my experiences, could be the key to helping others who are going through similar challenges."

Janet paused, her gaze settling on each of the students in turn, her expression radiating warmth and understanding. "That's why I wanted to create this group – a place where we can come together, support one another, and find the courage to stand up to the bullies and the self-doubt that try to hold us back."

As she spoke, Janet could see the glimmer of hope dawning on the faces of her peers, their eyes shining with a newfound sense of connection and purpose. And in that moment, she knew that this was more than just a support group – it was a sanctuary, a community of kindred spirits who were ready to embark on their own transformative journeys.

Janet felt a surge of pride and humility swell within her. In helping these students find their voices, she was continuing to heal and empower herself, coming full circle in the remarkable journey that had brought her to this pivotal moment.

With a warm smile, she gestured to the chairs, inviting the group to take a seat and share their stories. "So, who wants to go first?" she asked, her tone laced with a genuine curiosity and eagerness to listen.

As the students began to open up, their words laced with vulnerability and a sense of trust, Janet knew that this was just the beginning. The road ahead would undoubtedly be paved with challenges, but in this moment, she felt a profound sense of purpose and conviction – a belief that by uplifting and empowering others, she would continue to transform herself, one step at a time.

EMBRACING THE FUTURE

Janet stood before her graduating class, her heart pounding with a mix of nerves and determination. As she gazed out at the sea of familiar faces, she took a deep, steadying breath, allowing the weight of the moment to settle over her.

This was it – the culmination of a transformative journey that had once seemed impossible. Janet remembered the shy, insecure girl she had been, but that girl was no more.

With a quiet confidence that belied her once-timid nature, Janet began to speak, her voice strong and clear. "My fellow graduates, it is with great pride and humility that I stand before you today." She paused, allowing the words to hang in the air, the audience leaning in, captivated by the raw emotion in her tone.

"Four years ago, I was a girl who struggled to find her voice, to believe in her own worth. I was the target of relentless bullying, both from my peers and my own family." Janet's gaze swept across the sea of faces, meeting the eyes of her brothers, who sat with expressions of shame and remorse.

"But something changed. Through the support of my friends, the guidance of caring mentors, and the transformative power of the theater, I discovered the strength to stand up, to speak out, and to embrace the person I was always meant to be." Her voice grew stronger with each passing word, the conviction in her tone stirring the audience.

"I know that many of you have faced your own battles, your own struggles to find your place in this world. But I'm here to tell you that your voice matters. Your story matters. And the journey of self-discovery you've embarked upon is one of the most courageous and powerful things you can undertake."

Janet paused, her eyes glistening with unshed tears. "I stand before you today, not as the shy, insecure girl I once was, but as a young woman who has learned to embrace her unique identity, to find the power in her own voice. And I challenge each of you to do the same."

The audience erupted in thunderous applause, many wiping away tears as Janet's words resonated in their hearts. She had given voice to the struggles they had faced, the battles they had fought, and the transformations they had undergone. In that moment, she knew that her story had the power to inspire, to uplift, and to remind her fellow graduates that they were not alone in their journey.

As the applause faded, Janet caught the eye of her brothers, who sat with expressions of profound remorse and respect. She offered them a small, tentative smile, a silent acknowledgment of the progress they had made in repairing their fractured relationship.

With a deep breath, Janet turned her gaze back to the audience, her heart swelling with a mix of pride, gratitude, and excitement for the future. "Thank you, my friends, for allowing me to share my story. Now, let us go forth and continue to write the next chapter of our lives, with courage, with compassion, and with the strong belief that our voices can change the world."

The crowd erupted in thunderous applause once more, the air thick with a palpable energy of hope and possibility. Janet stood tall, her once-timid frame now radiating a quiet strength, a confirmation to the transformative power of finding one's voice. The applause faded, and Janet was surrounded by a swarm of well-wishers, each eager to offer their congratulations and share in the celebratory atmosphere.

Her theater friends, their faces alight with pride, enveloped her in a group hug, their laughter and excited chatter filling the air. "Janet, that was incredible!" one of them exclaimed, her eyes shining with admiration. "You were so powerful up there – I'm not ashamed to say I had a few tears in my eyes."

Janet felt a warm smile spread across her face as she basked in the genuine support of her theater family. These were the people who had witnessed her transformation, who had stood by her side as she found the courage to step into the spotlight and share her story with the world.

And then, to her surprise, her brothers approached her. Their expressions were a far cry from the taunting, dismissive looks she had once endured. The eldest brother, his gaze sheepish, offered a tentative smile. "Hey, Janet," he began, his voice uncharacteristically soft. "That was... that was really something. I'm – we're – proud of you."

Janet felt a flicker of astonishment cross her features as she took in the shift in her brothers' demeanor. Gone were the jeers and the cruel laughter, replaced by a genuine sense of respect and admiration. She exchanged a glance with her youngest brother, who nodded solemnly, his eyes shining with understanding.

In that moment, she was struck by the realization of just how far they had come. The confrontation that had once seemed so daunting, so fraught with pain and resentment, had paved the way for a profound transformation within their family. Through the difficult but necessary dialogue, they had begun to heal the fractures that had long divided them.

As her brothers offered their congratulations, Janet felt a weight lift from her shoulders being replaced by a sense of pride and self-acceptance. She had found her voice, and in doing so, she had inspired those closest to her to confront their own demons.

Liam, ever the supportive presence in her life, stood nearby, his eyes crinkling with a warm smile. When their gazes met, Janet felt a surge of gratitude wash over her. It was his unconditional belief in her, his gentle encouragement, that had played such a pivotal role in her transformation. Without him, she might never have found the courage to step into the spotlight and share her story with the world.

As the celebratory atmosphere continued to swirl around her, Janet took a moment to pause and reflect. The path that had led her to this moment had been fraught with challenges, but she had emerged stronger, more resilient, and more confident in her own identity than ever before. And as she looked towards the future, she felt a profound sense of excitement and determination – a belief that the next chapter of her life would be one of continued growth, self-discovery, and the limitless possibilities that lay ahead. Amidst the celebratory chaos, Janet felt a gentle tug on her sleeve. Turning, she found Liam standing there, a warm smile on his face.

"Hey, can we step aside for a moment?" he asked, his voice soft and inviting. "I have something I want to give you."

Janet nodded, her curiosity piqued, and followed Liam to a quieter corner of the room. There, he presented her with a carefully wrapped gift, his expression a mix of excitement and apprehension.

"I wanted to give you this," he said, his words laced with a hint of nervousness. "As a way to... to commemorate our journey together."

Carefully, Janet unwrapped the gift, her breath catching in her throat as she revealed a beautifully crafted scrapbook. Her fingers traced the intricate cover, a collage of images and mementos that told the story of their friendship.

As she opened the book, a flood of memories washed over her – the first time they had met, the tentative steps they had taken to build their bond, the moments of laughter and triumph, the challenges they had faced and overcome together.

Janet felt a lump rise in her throat, her eyes brimming with tears of joy and gratitude. "Liam, this is... this is incredible," she breathed, her voice thick with emotion.

He reached out, his hand gently squeezing her arm. "I wanted you to have something to look back on," he said, his own eyes shining with a quiet understanding. "A reminder of how far you've come, and how much you've grown."

Janet nodded, her fingers reverently tracing the pages, pausing on the moments that had shaped her journey. She could see the transformation reflected in the images – the shy, insecure girl she had once been, gradually blossoming into the confident young woman she was today.

"Thank you," she whispered, her gaze meeting Liam's. "For every-thing. I don't know if I would have found the courage to be here without you."

Liam smiled, his expression warm and sincere. "You did that all on your own, Janet," he said softly. "I was just there to support you, to believe in you when you couldn't believe in yourself."

They stood there in a moment of quiet gratitude, both acknowl-edging the profound impact their friendship had had on their lives. In that instant, Janet felt a deep well of affection for the young man who had become her most trusted companion and supporter.

As they shared a look of mutual understanding, Janet knew that their bond would endure, a testament to the power of connection, empathy, and the transformative journey of self-discovery they had embarked upon together.

The graduation party was a whirlwind of activity, with friends, family, and faculty members mingling and celebrating the momentous occasion. But amidst the lively chatter and laughter, Janet was pulled aside by a group of underclassmen, their expres-sions a mix of reverence and gratitude.

"Janet, we just wanted to say thank you," one of the students, a shy-looking girl, began, her voice barely above a whisper. "The support group you started for bullying victims – it's made such a difference in our lives."

Janet felt a surge of surprise and pride wash over her as the students continued to share their stories, each one more heartfelt than the last. They spoke of the courage they had found in her example, the way her willingness to speak out and stand up for herself had inspired them to do the same.

"Before, we just felt so alone, like we were the only ones going through this," another student, a lanky boy with a kind smile, explained. "But your group gave us a safe space to share our experiences and realize that we weren't alone."

Janet listened, her heart swelling with a profound sense of purpose. She remembered the fear and uncertainty she had felt when first starting the support group. But in that moment, she knew that her efforts had been more than worthwhile.

"You've really changed the culture at our school, you know," the shy girl continued, her eyes shining with admiration. "People are starting to speak up, to stand up for each other. And it's all because of you."

As the students expressed their gratitude, Janet felt a deep sense of pride and fulfillment. Her journey had not only transformed her own life but had also had a profound impact on those around her.

"Thank you," Janet replied, her voice thick with emotion. "Knowing that I've been able to help even one person – it means the world to me."

The students beamed, their expressions radiating with confidence and self-assurance. Janet could see the ripple effect of her own transformation reflected in their faces, a testament to the power of finding one's voice and using it to uplift and empower others. She knew that her story, her willingness to confront her own demons and embrace her true self, had the power to inspire and change lives. And in that moment, she felt more determined than ever to continue using her voice to make a positive impact on the world around her.

The celebratory atmosphere of the graduation party was interrupted by the arrival of Janet's parents, their expressions a mix of excitement and pride.

"Janet, sweetheart, we have something for you," her mother said, her voice trembling with emotion as she handed her daughter a thick envelope.

Janet felt a flutter of curiosity as she accepted the package, her fingers tracing the emblem on the front. As she carefully opened the envelope, her eyes widened in disbelief at the contents – a letter of acceptance to a prestigious theater program at a renowned university.

"Mom, Dad, I... I don't understand," Janet stammered, her voice barely above a whisper. "How is this possible?"

Her parents exchanged a warm, knowing glance, their faces alight with joy.

"We've been so impressed by the transformation we've seen in you, Janet," her father began, his hand coming to rest gently on her shoulder. "The courage and determination you've shown in pursuing your passion – it's truly inspiring."

Janet felt a lump rise in her throat as she listened to her father's words, her mind racing with a whirlwind of emotions. The future she had once believed to be out of reach was now within her grasp, a testament to the journey of self-discovery she had undertaken.

"We're so proud of you, honey," her mother added, her eyes shining with unshed tears. "You've overcome so much, and you've emerged stronger and more resilient than ever before."

As her parents enveloped her in a warm embrace, Janet felt a sense of wonder wash over her. She was now a confident young woman, ready to take on the world and chase her dreams with determination.

"Thank you," she murmured, her voice thick with emotion. "For believing in me, even when I didn't believe in myself."

Her parents smiled, their expressions radiating a profound sense of love and pride.

"You did this, Janet," her father said, his gaze filled with a quiet reverence. "We're just honored to have been a part of your journey."

In that moment, Janet felt a renewed sense of purpose and excitement for the future. The challenges she had faced, the battles she had fought, had all led her to this pivotal crossroads – a future filled with endless possibilities, where she could continue to use her voice to inspire, empower, and make a lasting impact on the world around her.

As the lively energy of the graduation party continued to swirl around her, she felt the need to step away, to find a moment of solitude and reflection. Quietly, she slipped out of the crowded room, her feet guiding her to a familiar destination – the community theater where her transformative journey had begun.

The doors creaked open, and she stepped into the dimly lit space, her senses immediately flooded with a rush of memories. She could almost hear the echoes of her first audition, the trembling in her voice as she nervously recited her lines. And there, on the stage, she recalled the pounding of her heart before the opening night performance, the exhilaration of finding her voice and sharing it with the world.

Slowly, Janet made her way to the center of the stage, her fingers tracing the worn wooden boards beneath her feet. This was where it all started – the place where she had discovered the power of self-expression, the courage to confront her fears and embrace her true self.

Closing her eyes, she took a deep, steadying breath, allowing the energy of the space to wash over her. And then, without a moment's hesitation, she began to speak, her voice resonating through the empty theater.

"To be, or not to be – that is the question," she recited, the familiar words of Hamlet's soliloquy flowing from her lips with a newfound confidence and conviction.

As she continued, Janet felt a surge of emotion swell within her, the weight of her journey etched in every syllable. She had come so far to be the young woman who now commanded the attention of an invisible audience.

Her voice echoed through the space. And in that moment, Janet felt a profound gratitude – for the mentors who had believed in her, the friends who had supported her, and the family who had ultimately learned to embrace her unique identity.

When the final words had faded into silence, she stood there, her heart pounding with a mix of exhilaration and nostalgia. This theater, this stage, had been the catalyst for her journey of self-discovery, the place where she had first found the courage to let her voice be heard.

With a small, wistful smile, Janet turned and made her way back towards the party, her steps lighter, her spirit renewed. The challenges that had once seemed insurmountable were now a distant memory, replaced by a deep sense of purpose and a burning desire to continue using her voice to inspire and empower those around her. As the evening drew to a close, she made her way back to the familiar comfort of her home, her mind still reeling from the whirlwind of emotions and experiences that had filled the day.

Stepping into her bedroom, she was immediately struck by the sight that greeted her – the walls adorned with an array of colorful, handwritten notes, each one confirming the impact she had made on the lives of those around her.

Janet felt a lump rise in her throat as she slowly made her way across the room, her fingers tracing the delicate messages, her eyes drinking in the words of gratitude, admiration, and inspiration.

Some of the notes were from her closest friends, the ones who had stood by her side throughout her journey of self-discovery. They spoke of the courage she had shown, the way her willingness to embrace her true self had inspired them to do the same.

But there were also messages from unexpected sources – classmates who had once been part of the taunting, jeering crowd, their words now laced with remorse and a newfound respect. They thanked Janet for her bravery, for using her voice to challenge the toxic culture that had once permeated the halls of their school.

And then, to Janet's surprise, she recognized the familiar scrawl of her brothers' handwriting, each message a heartfelt apology and an acknowledgment of the pain they had caused. Their words were tinged with a profound sense of regret, a recognition of how their actions had once wounded her, and a sincere desire to make amends.

As Janet read through the notes, her eyes brimming with tears, she was struck by the realization that her journey had touched so many lives in ways she had never imagined. Her willingness to confront her own demons, to stand up and share her story, had not only transformed her own life but had also inspired those around her to find the courage to do the same.

The weight of this revelation settled upon her, a profound sense of humility and gratitude washing over her. She had once believed that her voice was insignificant, that her experiences were too small to matter. But now, surrounded by the tangible evidence of the impact she had made, she knew that her story had the power to change lives, to uplift and empower those who had once felt just as lost and alone as she had.

With a deep, steadying breath, she carefully gathered the notes, clutching them to her chest as she sank down onto the edge of her bed. In that moment, she felt a renewed sense of purpose, a burning desire to continue using her voice to make a positive difference in the world. For her journey had only just begun, and the future that lay ahead was filled with endless possibilities.

As the night drew to a close, Janet was drawn to the familiar comfort of her desk, the well-worn journal that had accompanied her on her journey of self-discovery open before her.

With a deep, steadying breath, she picked up her pen, the weight of the moment settling upon her. This would be the final entry in a book that had become a repository for her innermost thoughts, a safe haven where she had poured out her fears, her struggles, and her hard-won triumphs.

Janet's fingers traced the pages, her eyes drifting over the words that had once seemed so foreign, so difficult to express. But now, as she prepared to embark on the next chapter of her life, those words held a newfound power.

She thought back to the shy, insecure girl she had once been, the one who had shrunk from the cruel taunts of her peers and the relentless bullying of her own brothers. That girl had been so consumed by self-doubt, so paralyzed by the fear of judgment and rejection, that the very idea of finding her voice had seemed like an impossible dream.

And yet, here she was, a young woman brimming with confidence, her spirit renewed by the challenges she had faced and the battles she had won. The road had not been an easy one, but with the support of her friends, the guidance of her mentors, and the belief of those who had seen her potential, she had emerged stronger, more resilient, and more in touch with her true self than ever before.

As she put pen to paper, the words flowed easily, a reflection of the growth and self-discovery she had experienced. She wrote of the friendships she had forged, the connections that had become the bedrock of her support system. She spoke of the exhilaration of stepping onto the stage, of finding the courage to share her voice with the world, and the profound sense of purpose that had blossomed within her.

And then, with a bittersweet smile, Janet turned her thoughts to the future, the next chapter that lay before her. College, with all its promises and challenges, beckoned, and she felt a surge of excitement and trepidation at the prospect. But this time, she was no longer the timid, insecure girl she had once been. She was a young woman who had faced her demons and had learned to embrace her unique identity. Someone who was ready to take on whatever obstacles lay ahead.

With a final, reverent stroke of her pen, Janet closed the journal, the weight of its pages a tangible reminder of the journey she had undertaken. As she gazed out the window, watching the world beyond her familiar surroundings, she felt a deep sense of gratitude.

Tomorrow, she would embark on a new adventure, one that would undoubtedly bring its own set of challenges and triumphs. But this time, Janet knew that she was more than ready to face them, her voice stronger, her spirit more resilient than ever before.

EPILOGUE - A LASTING IMPACT

Janet stood on the small stage in the school's auditorium, her gaze sweeping across the diverse group of students gathered before her. The familiar faces of her support group were interspersed with newcomers, all eyes fixed on her with rapt attention. Gone was that timid, self-conscious girl who struggled to find her voice. She was now a young woman with radiating confidence and purpose.

With a deep, steadying breath, she began to speak with words resonating with strength and clarity. "My friends, we have come a long way together. When I first started this support group, I was a girl consumed by insecurity, haunted by the cruel taunts of my peers and the relentless bullying of my own family."

A hush fell over the auditorium as Janet's voice carried through the space, her honesty and vulnerability captivating the audience. "But something changed. Through the power of community, the transformative experience of theater, and the support of those who believed in me, I found the courage to stand up, to speak out, and to embrace the person I was always meant to be."

Janet paused, she looked at the sea of faces, some familiar, some new. "I know that many of you have faced your own battles, your own struggles to find your place in this world. But I'm here to tell you that your voice matters. Your story matters. And the journey of self-discovery you've embarked upon is one of the most courageous and powerful things you can undertake."

Her words, once tentative and halting, now flowed with conviction, weaving together the threads of her own experiences – the theater that had unlocked her creativity, the confrontation with her brothers that had catalyzed her growth, and the support group that had become a sanctuary for those seeking to find their voice.

"I stand before you today, not as the shy, insecure girl I once was, but as a young woman who has learned to embrace her unique identity, to find the power in her own voice." Janet's eyes glistened with unshed tears, her expression a blend of pride and humility. "And I challenge each of you to do the same."

The auditorium erupted in thunderous applause, the energy in the room palpable as Janet's words resonated with the students. Many wiped away tears, their faces alight with a sense of inspiration and determination. Janet had given voice to the struggles they had faced, the battles they had fought, and the transformations they had undergone. In that moment, she knew that her story had the power to uplift and empower those who had once felt just as lost and alone as she had.

As the applause faded, Janet caught the eye of her brothers, who sat with expressions of profound remorse and respect. She offered them a small, tentative smile, a silent acknowledgment of the progress they had made in repairing their fractured relationship. The journey had not been an easy one, but through the difficult yet necessary dialogue, they had begun to heal the wounds of the past and forge a stronger, more understanding bond.

With a deep breath, Janet turned her gaze back to the audience, her heart swelling with a mix of pride, gratitude, and excitement for the future. "Thank you, my friends, for allowing me to share my story. Now, let us go forth and continue to write the next chapter of our lives, with courage, with compassion, and with the unwavering belief that our voices can change the world."

The crowd erupted in thunderous applause once more, the air thick with a palpable energy of hope and possibility. Janet stood tall, her once-timid frame now radiating a quiet strength, a testament to the transformative power of finding one's voice. In that moment, she knew that her journey had only just begun, and the future that lay ahead was filled with endless opportunities to inspire, empower, and make a lasting impact on the world around her.

As Janet's powerful words faded, a hush fell over the auditorium. For a moment, the students seemed almost reluctant to break the spell she had cast, the weight of her journey still palpable in the air. Then, with a tentative step forward, a shy freshman boy emerged from the crowd, his voice barely audible at first. "I-I'd like to share something, if that's okay," he murmured, his gaze fixed on the floor.

Janet offered him an encouraging smile, her expression warm and welcoming. "Of course," she replied softly. "The floor is yours."

Slowly, the boy's story began to unfold, his words gaining strength and conviction as he spoke. He recounted the relentless torment he had endured through cyberbullying, the cruel messages and taunts that had chipped away at his self-worth, leaving him feeling isolated and alone.

As he spoke, Janet listened intently, her eyes shining with empathy. Reaching out, she gently placed a hand on the boy's arm, offering a silent gesture of support that seemed to steady his trembling voice.

One by one, other students followed the freshman's lead, each stepping forward to share their own unique struggles and triumphs. A girl described the pain of being shunned by her peers for her disability, while a boy spoke of the crippling anxiety that had once held him back.

The atmosphere in the auditorium shifted, the air charged with a palpable sense of vulnerability and mutual understanding. Gone were the social barriers and hierarchies that had once divided the students – in their place, a community of empathy and support had blossomed, each person's stories coming together in this journey.

Janet listened, her heart swelling with a profound sense of purpose. These were the voices she had fought to amplify, the stories she had longed to bring to light. And in that moment, she knew that her work was far from over – that the support group she had founded was just the beginning of a movement that would continue to inspire and empower those who had once felt lost and alone.

As the sharing session drew to a close, Janet could sense a shift in the energy of the room. The students, once timid and guarded, now radiated with confidence, their eyes shining with a glimmer of hope. It was at this moment that Janet knew the true impact of her journey – not just on her own life, but on the lives of those around her.

As the sharing session drew to a close, she noticed a group of students she had never seen at the support group meetings before. They were the kind of kids she had once envied, the popular crowd who seemed to glide effortlessly through the halls of the school, untouched by the insecurities and struggles that had consumed her own life.

Yet, as the students approached her during the break, their expressions were not ones of indifference or disdain, but rather a mix of admiration and vulnerability. Janet watched, her curiosity piqued, as they hesitantly made their way towards her.

"Hey, Janet," one of the girls began, her voice soft and tentative. "We, um, we just wanted to say that what you're doing here – it's really amazing. And, well, we kind of admire your courage."

Janet felt surprised, her eyes widening as the girl's words sank in. These were the very students who had once been part of the jeering, taunting crowd, the ones who had contributed to the toxic culture that had once permeated the halls of their school.

"Courage?" Janet echoed, her brow furrowing in confusion. "I don't understand. Why would you –"

Another student, a tall boy with a sheepish expression, stepped forward, cutting her off. "The truth is, we all kind of have our own insecurities, you know?" He admitted. His gaze shifted nervously. "And seeing you stand up like this, it's – it's really inspiring."

Janet stood there, momentarily at a loss for words, as the group of popular students continued to open up, their voices laced with a vulnerability she had never expected to witness. They spoke of the pressure to maintain a certain image, the constant fear of judgment and rejection, and the deep-seated insecurities that lurked beneath the surface of their seemingly confident exteriors.

In that moment, Janet felt a profound shift in the group dynamic, as long-standing social barriers began to crumble. The students who had once seemed so untouchable, so far removed from the struggles she had faced, were now baring their hearts, their shared humanity transcending the artificial divisions that had once defined their world.

As Janet listened, she realized the true power of her journey – not just in transforming her own life, but in creating a ripple effect that had the potential to reach even the most unexpected corners of the school community. Her willingness to confront her demons and embrace her true self had opened the door for others to do the same, shattering the illusion of perfection and inviting a deeper level of empathy and understanding.

With a gentle smile, Janet reached out, placing a hand on the arm of the girl who had first spoken. "Thank you," she said, her voice thick with emotion. "For being here, for sharing your stories. It means more than you know."

The students nodded, their faces alight with a sense of connection and camaraderie. In that moment, she knew that the support group she had founded had become so much more than just a safe haven for the bullied and the broken – it was a catalyst for transformation, a space where the walls of social hierarchy could crumble, and the true power of community could be unleashed. As the vulnerable sharing session drew to a close, she felt a shift in the energy of the room. Seizing the moment, she guided the group into a series of exercises inspired by her own transformative experiences in the theater.

"Let's try something a little different, she announced," her voice carrying a note of excitement. "I want you all to pair up and get ready for some trust-building activities."

The students exchanged curious glances, but quickly complied, pairing off and turning to face one another. Janet moved among the pairs, her eyes sparkling with a contagious enthusiasm.

"Alright," she began, her tone warm and encouraging. "I want one of you to close your eyes and fall back, trusting your partner to catch you. Go on, give it a try!"

At first, the students were tentative, their movements stiff and uncertain. But as they began to surrender to the exercise, a shift occurred. Laughter and giggles filled the air as they discovered the joy of relinquishing control and placing their trust in another person.

Janet beamed, her heart swelling with pride as she observed the transformation unfolding before her. With gentle guidance and words of encouragement, she moved from pair to pair, offering gentle nudges and reminders to let go and embrace the experience.

The room buzzed with a palpable sense of connection, the students' initial hesitation melting away as they immersed themselves in the trust-building activities. Janet watched, her natural leadership shining through, as they moved on to mirroring exercises, their movements synchronized in a captivating dance of empathy and understanding.

As the workshop drew to a close, Janet gathered the group, her expression radiant. "You all did an incredible job today," she praised, her gaze sweeping across the sea of faces. "I'm so proud of the courage and vulnerability you've shown."

The students erupted in applause, their faces alight with a sense of camaraderie and self-assurance. Janet basked in the moment, her own transformation reflected in the transformation of those around her. This support group, once a sanctuary for the broken and the bullied, had blossomed into a vibrant community of empowerment, where the power of connection and self-expression had the ability to heal and uplift.

Janet knew that her journey was far from over. The road ahead was still paved with challenges and uncertainties, but she was no longer the timid, insecure girl she had once been. She was ready to continue using her voice to inspire, to empower, and to create a lasting impact on the world around her. As the energetic workshop activities drew to a close, Janet turned to the group, her expression alight with excitement and said "I have one more surprise for all of you today," her voice carrying a note of anticipation.

The students leaned in, their curiosity piqued, as Janet gestured towards the back of the auditorium. "Please welcome our special guest," she said warmly, stepping aside to reveal a poised, middle-aged woman with a kind, welcoming demeanor.

"This is Dr. Emerson, a local therapist who specializes in teen issues," Janet explained. "She's here to share some insights and advice that I hope will complement the work we've been doing in our support group."

A hush fell over the audience as Dr. Emerson stepped forward, her gaze sweeping across the attentive faces. "It's a pleasure to be here with all of you today," she began, her voice carrying a soothing, professional tone. "I've been so inspired by the courage and vulnerability I've witnessed in this room."

The students listened intently as the therapist shared her expertise, her words offering a valuable complement to the peer-led approach Janet had cultivated. She spoke of the importance of building self-esteem, of developing healthy coping mechanisms to deal with the challenges of adolescence, and of the transformative power of finding one's voice.

As she concluded her insights, Dr. Emerson turned to the group, her expression warm and inviting. "Now, I'd like to open the floor to any questions you might have. I'm here to listen and to provide any guidance or support I can offer."

Hands shot up eagerly, and soon the auditorium was filled with the students' queries, each one revealing the unique struggles and concerns they faced. A shy freshman asked about strategies for dealing with cyberbullying, while a confident-looking girl inquired about the best ways to support a friend who was experiencing anxiety.

Janet watched, her heart swelling with pride, as the students engaged with the therapist, their questions and responses showcasing the depth of their personal journeys. Gone were the days of timid silence and avoidance – in their place, a palpable sense of determination and a hunger for growth had blossomed.

As the Q&A session drew to a close, Dr. Emerson offered the group a warm smile. "Remember," she said gently, "you are not alone in this. The challenges you face may seem daunting, but with the right support and the courage to confront them, you have the power to overcome anything."

The students erupted in applause, their faces alight with a renewed sense of hope and resolve. Janet knew that the insights shared by the therapist, combined with the peer-led approach of the support group, had the potential to create a powerful synergy – one that would continue to empower and uplift the young people in her community.

As the meeting adjourned, Janet was surrounded by so many grateful faces, each one offering a heartfelt expression of thanks. In that moment, she felt a profound sense of purpose, a realization that her journey had become so much more than just her own – it was a catalyst for transformative change, a ripple effect that was spreading far beyond the confines of the auditorium. As the students filed out of the auditorium, buzzing with the energy of the Q&A session, Janet called them back, her expression solemn yet purposeful.

"Before we go, I have one more thing I'd like us to do together," she announced, her voice carrying a note of gravity.

The students turned their attention to her, their curiosity piqued. Janet moved to a table at the front of the room, retrieving a stack of paper and a collection of pens.

"I want each of you to take a moment and write down a fear or insecurity that you've been carrying," she explained, her gaze sweeping across the group. "Something that's been holding you back, something you're ready to let go of."

The students exchanged uncertain glances, but one by one, they approached the table, each claiming a slip of paper and a pen. Janet watched as they bent over the pages, their expressions a mix of vulnerability and determination.

When they had all finished, Janet gestured to a large glass jar standing nearby. "Now, I want you to come up one by one and tear up your paper," she instructed, her voice soft yet resolute. "Symbolically release that fear, that insecurity, and let it go."

The students hesitated for a moment, then began to approach the jar, their movements tentative at first. But as the first scrap of paper was torn and dropped into the container, a shift occurred. The action seemed to unleash a wave of catharsis, and soon the air was filled with the sound of tearing paper and the occasional sniffle.

Janet moved among the students, offering gentle encouragement and a reassuring presence as they confronted their deepest vulnerabilities. She watched, her heart swelling with emotion, as the jar slowly filled with the discarded remnants of their fears and insecurities.

When the last student had released their paper, Janet placed a lid on the jar, her gaze thoughtful. "This, she said solemnly, will be the foundation of a collaborative art project we'll be working on in the coming weeks." A visual representation of our collective journey – the struggles we've faced, the burdens we've carried, and the growth we've achieved."

The students stood in silence, their eyes glistening with unshed tears. The ritual had been a profoundly cathartic experience, a tangible release of the weight they had been bearing.

As the students began to file out, their steps lighter and their expressions more serene, Janet felt a deep sense of pride and purpose. This was the legacy she hoped to leave behind – a community of empowered individuals, each one stronger and more resilient than the last, united in their journey of self-discovery and growth.

As the last of the students filtered out of the auditorium, Janet began to gather the materials from the meeting, her mind still buzzing with the powerful energy that had filled the space. She was just about to head for the door when a familiar voice called out to her.

"Janet, a moment of your time, please?"

Turning, she found the school principal approaching, his expression one of deep contemplation. She felt a flutter of apprehension, wondering if she had somehow overstepped her bounds or caused a disturbance. But as the principal drew closer, his features softened into a warm smile.

"I've been observing your support group meetings for some time now," he began, his gaze carrying a note of admiration. "And I have to say, Janet, I'm incredibly impressed by the work you've been doing here."

Janet felt a surge of surprise, her eyes widening as the principal's words sank in. She opened her mouth to respond, but he raised a hand, gently cutting her off.

"The way you've been able to create a safe space for these students, to empower them to find their voices – it's truly remarkable. And I think it's time we take this initiative to the next level."

Janet felt a mix of pride and trepidation wash over her. "Next level?" she echoed, her brow furrowing in uncertainty.

The principal nodded, his expression resolute. "I'd like to propose expanding your support group into a school-wide program," he explained, his tone brimming with enthusiasm. "We could offer it as an elective course, with you at the helm, and bring in additional resources and expertise to complement your peer-led approach."

Janet felt her heart begin to race, the weight of the principal's words settling upon her. "A school-wide program?" She had never imagined her modest support group would grow to such proportions, and the prospect both thrilled and terrified her.

"I-I'm not sure what to say," she stammered, her gaze shifting nervously. "This is all so... unexpected."

The principal placed a reassuring hand on her shoulder, his eyes shining with conviction. "Janet, you've already made such a profound impact on this community. Imagine what you could do if we expanded the reach of this initiative."

Janet felt a surge of responsibility wash over her, a realization that her personal journey had the power to transform the lives of so many more students. She thought of the vulnerable faces she had witnessed today, the stories of pain and resilience that had unfolded within these walls. The thought of being able to offer that same lifeline to a wider audience filled her with a sense of purpose and determination.

Slowly, a smile spread across her face, and she nodded, her expression resolute. "I'm in," she said. "Let's do this."

The principal beamed, his hand giving her shoulder a gentle squeeze. "Wonderful," he exclaimed. "I'll start making the arrangements right away. This is going to be something truly special, Janet. I can feel it."

As the principal strode away, Janet stood there, a mix of emotions swirling within her. The responsibility was daunting, but the prospect of reaching and empowering even more young people filled her with a profound sense of excitement. Her journey had come so far, and now, it was poised to have an impact that extended far beyond her own personal growth.

With a deep, steadying breath, she gathered the remaining materials, her steps lighter and her spirit renewed. The road ahead might be filled with challenges, but she was no longer the timid, insecure girl she had once been. She was now a leader, a beacon of hope, and she was ready to continue using her voice to inspire and transform the lives of those around her. As Janet gathered the remaining materials from the support group meeting, her mind still reeling from the principal's proposal, she heard a familiar voice call out to her.

"Janet! There you are!"

Turning, she found Liam and a group of her theater friends approaching, their expressions alight with excitement. Janet felt a flutter of surprise, wondering what could have them all so energized.

"Hey, guys," she greeted, her brow furrowing in confusion. "What's going on?"

Liam stepped forward, a broad grin spreading across his face. "We have something to tell you," he announced, his eyes sparkling with pride. "You've been nominated for the Youth Leadership Award!"

Janet felt her breath catch in her throat, her eyes widening in disbelief. "What? I... I don't understand."

Her theater friends gathered around her, their voices overlapping as they showered her with congratulations and praise. "It's true, Janet!" one of the girls exclaimed, her face beaming. "The community organization recognized all the amazing work you've been doing with the support group and in the theater."

Janet stood there, momentarily speechless, as the reality of their words sank in. She had been so consumed by the challenges of her own journey, so focused on finding the courage to use her voice, that the idea of being recognized for her efforts had never even crossed her mind.

Liam placed a gentle hand on her arm, his expression warm and understanding. "You deserve this, Janet," he said softly. "You've come so far, and you've inspired so many people along the way."

As the weight of his words settled upon her, she felt a surge of emotion wash over her. She thought back to the timid, insecure girl she had once been, the one who had struggled to even raise her hand in class, let alone stand before a crowd and share her story. The transformation she had undergone felt nothing short of miraculous, a testament to the power of self-discovery and the unconditional support of those who believed in her.

Tears welled in her eyes as she looked around at the faces of her friends, each one beaming with pride and affection. "I don't know what to say," she murmured, her voice thick with emotion. "This is... this is incredible."

Liam pulled her into a warm embrace, his own eyes shining with unshed tears. "You should be proud of yourself, Janet," he whispered. "You've come so far, and you've touched so many lives in the process."

As Janet held onto Liam, feeling the support and love of her theater family surrounding her, she allowed herself a moment of quiet reflection. The journey that had once seemed so daunting, so fraught with challenges, had led her to this pivotal moment – a recognition of the strength and resilience she had cultivated, the courage she had found to confront her demons and embrace her true self.

In that instant, the insecure girl she had once been felt like a distant memory, a shadow of the confident, empowered young woman she had become. And as she basked in the warmth and admiration of those around her, she knew that this was only the beginning – that the future held endless possibilities for her to continue using her voice to inspire and uplift others.

As the celebratory atmosphere began to fade, Janet bid farewell to her theater friends and Liam, her heart still swelling with a mix of pride and gratitude. Gathering her belongings, she made her way out of the school, her steps lighter and her spirit renewed.

But as she approached the familiar path leading to her home, she noticed a figure standing in the distance, silhouetted against the fading evening light. Squinting, she felt a flutter of apprehension as she recognized the tall, lanky frame of one of her brothers.

Slowly, she approached, her mind racing with a thousand questions. What was he doing here, waiting for her?

As she drew closer, Janet was struck by the uncharacteristic expression on her brother's face – one of hesitation, and perhaps even a hint of remorse.

"Hey, Janet," he began, his voice soft and tentative. "Can we... can we talk for a minute?"

Janet felt a surge of uncertainty, her gaze searching his features for any sign of the cruel, dismissive boy she had once known. But to her surprise, she found only a glimmer of vulnerability and a quiet resolve.

"Uh, sure," she replied, her own voice carrying a note of caution. "What is it?"

Her brother took a deep breath, his hands fidgeting nervously. "I, um... I just wanted to say how proud I am of you," he admitted, his gaze meeting hers with sincerity. "What you've been doing, with the support group and everything – it's really amazing."

She felt her breath catch in her throat, her eyes widening in disbelief. "Proud?" she echoed, the word foreign on her tongue. "After all the... all the things you said to me?"

Her brother's expression darkened with a pained remorse, and he nodded solemnly. "I know," he murmured, his voice laced with regret. "I know I've said some awful things to you, and I can never take that back. But I... I want you to know that I'm sorry. I'm so, so sorry."

Janet stood there, momentarily at a loss for words, as her brother's apology washed over her. She had spent years harboring resentment and pain, convinced that her own family would never see her as anything more than the target of their cruel taunts. But now, as she gazed into his eyes, she saw a glimmer of the brother she had once known – the one who had played with her as children, before the weight of their family's expectations had driven them apart.

Slowly, a tentative smile spread across her face, and she reached out, placing a hand on his arm. "I forgive you," she said softly, her voice thick with emotion. "And... I'm proud of you, too. For being here, for saying this."

Her brother's expression shifted, a weight lifting from his shoulders as he pulled her into a hesitant embrace. "Thank you, Janet, he murmured, his voice barely above a whisper. Thank you for giving me another chance."

As they stood there, the tension and resentment slowly gave way to understanding, Janet felt a profound sense of gratitude. Her journey of self-discovery had not only transformed her own life, but had also catalyzed growth and healing within her family – a testament to the power of vulnerability, forgiveness, and the resilience of the human spirit.

With a deep, steadying breath, Janet pulled back, her gaze meeting her brother's with a quiet confidence. "Come on, she said," her voice warm and inviting. "Let's go home. I think it's time we had a real conversation."

Her brother nodded, a small smile tugging at the corners of his lips, and together they set off, the weight of the past slowly giving way to the promise of a brighter future – one where the bonds of family could be mended, and the scars of the past could finally heal.

Once at home, Janet was drawn to the familiar comfort of her desk, the well-worn journal that had accompanied her on her journey of self-discovery open before her. With a deep, steadying breath, she picked up her pen, her fingers tracing the weathered cover as she prepared to write her final entry about this chapter in her life.

The events of the day had been a whirlwind, a tapestry of emotions and experiences that had left her feeling both exhilarated and contemplative. She thought back to the timid, insecure girl she had once been, the one who had shrunk from the cruel taunts of her peers and the relentless bullying of her own family. That girl felt like a distant memory, a shadow of the confident, empowered young woman she had become.

As she began to write, the words flowed with a newfound fluency, a reflection of the growth and self-discovery she had undergone.

She recounted the pivotal moments that had shaped her journey – the chance encounter with Liam that had sparked her transformation, the cathartic experience of finding her voice on the stage, and the profound impact of confronting her brothers and reclaiming her place within their fractured family.

The power of finding one's voice, she wrote, her pen moving across the page with a sense of purpose, is a transformative force that can ripple outwards, touching the lives of those around us. I've seen it firsthand, in the faces of the students who have shared their stories in our support group, in the shift in the social dynamics of my own school community.

Janet paused, her gaze drifting out the window as she contemplated the far-reaching implications of her journey. What had once seemed like a solitary struggle had blossomed into a movement, a catalyst for change that had the potential to inspire and empower countless others who had once felt just as lost and alone as she had.

And it all started with me, she mused, a small, wistful smile tugging at the corners of her lips. The shy, bullied girl who found the courage to stand up, to speak out, and to embrace the person she was always meant to be.

Turning her attention back to the journal, Janet continued to write, her words infused with a profound sense of gratitude and purpose. This journey has been one of the most challenging and rewarding experiences of my life. It has tested me, pushed me to my limits, and forced me to confront the deepest parts of myself.

But in the end, she reflected, it has also given me the gift of self-discovery, of finding the strength to not only overcome my own demons but to inspire and uplift those around me. And as I look towards the future, I know that this is only the beginning – that the possibilities that lie ahead are endless, and that my voice, once timid and silenced, now has the power to change the world.

With a final flourish of her pen, Janet closed the journal, her heart swelling with a mix of pride, humility, and excitement for the journey that lay ahead. The road had been long and arduous, but she had emerged stronger, more resilient, and more confident in her own identity than ever before. And as she stood, her gaze fixed on the horizon, she knew that the future was hers to shape, one empowered word and one inspired life at a time. As the evening drew to a close, her was gaze fixed on the reflection staring back at her in the mirror. This was the same mirror that had once been a source of dread and self-loathing, the place where she had seen only the insecure, bullied girl she had once been.

But now, as she studied her features, she saw a transformation that went far beyond the physical. Her usual timid expression had been replaced by a quiet confidence, a resolute determination that shone in her eyes and the set of her jaw, a reflection of a young woman who had found the courage to confront the pain and insecurities that had consumed her before, a young woman who had emerged stronger and more in touch with her true self than ever before.

Clearing her throat, Janet began to speak with clarity and conviction. "To be, or not to be – that is the question," she recited, the familiar words of Hamlet's soliloquy flowing from her lips with a depth of meaning that had eluded her in the past.

As she continued, Janet wove together the themes that had defined her transformative journey – resilience in the face of adversity, the power of self-discovery, and the profound impact of community support.

"We all face battles, both within ourselves and in the world around us," she declared, her expression resolute. "But it is in those moments of darkness that we find the strength to rise, to confront our fears, and to embrace the person we were always meant to be."

Janet's words carried a weight that belied her years, a wisdom born of the challenges faced and the growth she had undergone. She spoke of the importance of finding your own voice and using that voice to inspire and empower those around you, and of the transformative ripple effect that could be unleashed when individuals dared to be their authentic selves.

As she rehearsed the speech, Janet saw echoes of the reflection of the various versions of herself that had led her to this pivotal moment. The timid, insecure girl who had once shrunk from the world, the determined young woman who had found the courage to step into the spotlight, and the confident, empowered leader she had become – all of these facets were woven into her transformative journey.

And as she gazed out at the future that stretched before her, Janet felt a profound sense of excitement and possibility. The road ahead was still paved with challenges and uncertainties, but she was no longer the same person who had once trembled at the thought of confronting her fears. She was a living testament to the power of self-discovery and the transformative impact that one voice could have on the world.

With a deep, steadying breath, Janet straightened her shoulders, her expression resolute. "Let us go forth," she declared, her voice ringing with conviction, "and continue to write the next chapter of her life, with courage and compassion, and with the firm belief that our voices can change the world."

As the final words faded, Janet allowed herself a moment of quiet reflection, a small, triumphant smile tugging at the corners of her lips. The journey had been long and arduous, but she had emerged stronger and resilient, and more in touch with her true self than ever before. And as she turned away from the mirror, her steps lighter and her spirit renewed, Janet knew that the future that lay ahead was filled with endless possibilities – a confirmation to the transformative power of finding your own voice and the limitless potential that resides within.

ABOUT THE AUTHOR

Janet M. Garcia

With a robust academic foundation in Sociology and Psychology, Janet is deeply passionate about understanding the complexities of human behavior.

Her passion to help others led her to write a series of books and novels on a variety of topics.

She aims to make a difference in the lives of struggling individuals, especially young people, using her vast knowledge and experiences.

Her mission is to help others find hope, strength, and solace in their journey. With her work, the author hopes to reduce the isolation and stresses that prevent young people from being who they are really meant to be.

LEAVE A 1-CLICK REVIEW

Customer Reviews

★★★★★ 2
5.0 out of 5 stars

5 star		100%
4 star		0%
3 star		0%
2 star		0%
1 star		0%

Share your thoughts with other customers

Write a customer review

See all verified purchase reviews ›

I would be incredibly thankful if you take just
60-seconds to write a brief review on Amazon,
even if it's just a few sentences!

https://amazon.com/review/create-review?asin=1960188399